MYSTERY OF THE MISSING HEIRESS

**Trixie
Belden**

Your TRIXIE BELDEN Library

Trixie Belden and the
MYSTERY OF THE MISSING HEIRESS

BY KATHRYN KENNY

Cover by Jack Wacker

GOLDEN PRESS

Western Publishing Company, Inc.

Racine, Wisconsin

CONTENTS

MYSTERY OF THE MISSING HEIRESS

Discovery at the Marsh • 1

"HONK THE HORN!" Trixie Belden called excitedly and put her hand over Brian's tanned fingers. With an older brother's tolerance, he smiled and stopped his battered, stripped-down car in front of the Manor House, the huge Wheeler estate at Sleepy-side-on-the-Hudson.

"If I know Honey and Jim," he said, "they've been looking out of a window for half an hour, rackets in hand, waiting for us."

"Maybe," Trixie said and jumped from the car. "They should be coming around the house right now if they heard the car."

Mart, almost her twin, swung his slim legs over

the doorless backseat. "Heck, they can hear it the minute Brian backs out of the garage, half a mile away."

"Hi!" they called to Tom, the Wheeler chauffeur, who was washing down the station wagon.

"Hi, yourselves!" Tom answered. Anyone could tell from the broad grin on his face that he liked the "Belden kids," as he called them—especially Trixie, his boss's daughter's best friend. It was so much fun to tease her. She had a temper, although her short, sandy curls and big blue eyes belied it.

"I'm trying to clean and polish this car so it'll look just the way you want it," Tom said. "I didn't think it would take long for you to get here, once you heard the news."

"What news?" Trixie asked breathlessly. "Hi, Honey! Hi, Jim! Are you going on a trip? Is that the news?"

Honey, a tall, graceful blonde just Trixie's age, came out of the house, smiling, followed by her older brother, Jim.

Tom threw down the hose in disgust. "Do you mean you Belden kids don't know what I'm talking about? Gosh, Honey, I sure opened my big mouth. Your dad will be plenty mad at me."

"No, he won't," said Honey, laughing. "Daddy never gets 'plenty mad' at anyone, without a very good reason."

"Then what did Tom mean?" Trixie insisted.

"Aren't we going to play tennis this morning?"

Jim just laughed. "Take a look in the garage!"

He watched Trixie, Brian, and Mart as their eyes widened in wonder at the brand-new Continental sedan, shiny and blue, glittering with chrome.

"Gol, it's neat!" Mart said, awed.

"Cool!" Brian echoed.

"Isn't she a beauty?" Tom asked, laying his hands lovingly on the hood. "She'll sure leave you far behind in the old station wagon, Jim."

"Are you going to drive the station wagon now, Jim?" Trixie asked with great interest.

"Not only drive it." Jim grew an inch taller before their eyes. "I'm part owner!"

"Is Honey the other part?" Trixie asked quickly. Then she added sadly, "She can't even drive."

"I'm one of the owners," Honey said excitedly. "You are, too, Trixie, and Brian and Mart and Diana and Dan!"

She giggled at the questions in their eyes. "Daddy is giving our station wagon to the Bob-Whites of the Glen."

"He's doing *what?*" Trixie asked, unbelieving. "Look at what Mart's doing!"

Mart, out of sheer joy at the news, turned cartwheel after cartwheel down the concrete drive.

At Trixie's words he stopped, dusted himself off, and stamped his foot, frustrated. "Why am I so steamed up? I won't be old enough to drive for another year. But, say—" he grinned impishly—"I sure can order my own limousine."

He turned to Jim, opened the station wagon's rear door with a flourish, stepped in, and commanded, "Home, James!"

The others laughed delightedly, ran around the car, patted it, and exclaimed, hardly daring to believe this glorious car could really be their very own.

Reddy, the Beldens' Irish setter, who had followed them from home, raced madly around the Bob-Whites, then skidded suddenly to a stop, tail wagging, wondering about the excitement and loving it all.

"Let's take a spin down Glen Road," Trixie called, "and sound the horn all the way. Beep! Beep! Honk! Honk! Come on, gang. Who'll drive, Jim or Brian?"

"You drive," Jim told his friend generously and opened the door to the driver's seat.

"Nope . . . *you*," Brian protested. "I have to wheel my old jalopy out of the drive, anyway."

He gave his old car a loving push, remembering the agony they all went through to earn the fifty dollars it had cost months before. "We'll have to stop at Di's, then hunt up Dan and tell him. Hi, Regan!"

Regan, the Wheelers' groom and one of the Bob-Whites' very best friends, came out of the stable and over to the station wagon.

Because Mr. and Mrs. Wheeler had to be away much of the time, Regan kept Honey and Jim in line. He extended his advice to include the Belden young people, too, when they were around the Wheeler estate. None of them resented his discipline. It always was just.

They didn't resent it now when, as they were about to take off in their new car, Regan said soberly, "The car's swell. I'm glad you have it—but *it* doesn't have to be exercised. Inside the stable"— he gestured with his thumb—"I have five riding horses begging to be taken out . . . pawing and restless. That's the first order of business. Right, kids? Don't forget the Turf Show next month!"

Reluctantly but understandingly, they nodded their heads. *Any other day,* Trixie thought, *just any other day. . . .*

"Okay, Regan," she said aloud as they all walked toward the stable. "You win. But, jeepers, it'll be forever before we get to try out our new car. When we come back, we'll have to groom the horses, clean the tack—"

"One thing at a time, Miss Fidget!" A smile curved around Regan's mouth. "I just might help."

"You nearly always do," Trixie said, ashamed. "Shall I ride Susie today?" She stroked the little black mare's soft nose.

"If you will, please, Trixie. You ride well enough

now, though, that you could almost have your choice of horses." Regan never was lavish with his praise, and Trixie colored.

"You can't ride Jupiter!" Jim warned as he saddled the mettlesome black gelding. "Brian's the only one who rides him, except me."

"You forget Daddy," Honey reminded him. "Jupiter's really his horse." She swept her hand around, indicating the walls of the tack room. "Look at the ribbons he's taken for jumping! Oh, well, I'll take Lady, any day." At the sound of Honey's voice, the beautiful gray mare raised her head.

"That leaves Starlight for Brian and Strawberry for me," Mart said. "Go back home, Reddy! Home!"

He might as well have spoken to the wind. Reddy ran yapping into the shrubbery, only to come galumphing back, mouth drooling, brown eyes begging: *You do want me, don't you?*

Honey laughed. "You may as well give in, Mart. Patch always goes. He's Jim's shadow." The springer spaniel, hearing his name, upped his big ears and whimpered. Honey bent to stroke his wriggling body. "The dogs love the woods as much as we do."

"Shall we go past Di's house first and tell her the news about the car, then pick up Dan at Mr. Maypenny's cottage?"

The woods, a huge game preserve, was only a

small part of the Wheeler estate with its private lake for swimming, its fine stable, and its paddock. The preserve was the place the Bob-Whites liked best to ride. It was deep, dark, and mysterious, with trails crossing and recrossing. There were parts of it, still unexplored, where deer and foxes roamed. On rare occasions even a catamount found its way down from the Catskills. The west boundary ended only ten feet from the edge of the great bluffs that hung over the Hudson River.

Jim rode ahead as they left Manor House. The others followed him down the path that would take them past Crabapple Farm, the Beldens' clapboarded old home, which was wrapped cozily in orchards ripe with fruit. It was a modest home compared to the large estates which had grown up around it over the years. Three generations of Beldens had lived here, adding rooms as needed. Now it sprawled, gracious and hospitable, in the midst of rose and vegetable gardens, chicken runs, and berry patches.

From inside the farm's white picket fence, Bobby, the youngest Belden, a first grader, waved as the Bob-Whites passed. He whistled to Reddy, who ignored his little master to follow the horses.

"I'll be glad when Bobby is old enough to ride with us," Trixie thought as she looked back at her small brother's dejected form. "It doesn't seem right. . . ."

In the driveway of Diana Lynch's great stone home, they reined in their horses and whistled the clear club call: *bob, bob-white!*

Around the corner of the exercise yard, a silver and gold palomino raised his head and whinnied. Diana, a beautiful girl with shining black shoulder-length hair, wearing tan jodhpurs, answered the whistle: *bob-white! bob, bob-white!* and ran out.

"I knew you were coming. Miss Trask called me."

"She did?" Honey asked. "She fixed some sandwiches for us to take along. Isn't she a dear? Did she tell you anything?"

"Just that you were riding and wanted me to go with you. I've saddled Sunny. Say . . . what *could* Miss Trask have told me? Why are you all grinning? Tell me!"

Mart urged Strawberry over closer to Diana and brushed his hand nonchalantly over his short, sandy hair. "It's nothing . . . really nothing . . . it's just. . . ."

"That the Bob-Whites have their very own car!" Trixie exploded. "A station wagon!"

"Now, where in the world would we ever get anything like that? You have to be fooling. I'm not old enough to drive. You aren't, Trixie. Honey isn't, either, or Mart. Where would we get a car?" she repeated. "Where?"

"Honey and Jim's father," Trixie said dramatically. "He has a marvelous new Lincoln Continental and has given his old car to the Bob-Whites. Did you ever hear of anything like that? Jim's going to paint our club name on the door. Who'll drive it? Why, Jim and Brian, for now, and Dan will learn. But it belongs to every one of us! Oh, hurry, Di. We're going to the gamekeeper's cottage to tell Dan the news, too."

Diana didn't move. "I just can't believe it!" she gasped. "It's too—too—too super! Why, even the Sleepyside Turf Club doesn't own a car!"

"Why speak of that unimportant organization in the same breath with the Bob-Whites of the Glen?" Mart asked. "Gol, when I think of all that's happened to us in the past year or so. . . ."

"Ever since Honey's family moved to Manor House," Trixie added, "and Di's family moved here —and Dan!"

"We have the best club in the United States of America," Honey said. "I *always* wanted to belong to a club like ours."

Trixie nodded her head. "Now all seven of us belong."

"With a clubhouse thrown in," Brian reminded her.

"Which we broke our backs mending and rebuilding and furnishing—" Mart stopped when he saw Trixie's face.

"Mart Belden! We're the luckiest people in the

whole world! Just think of it—the Wheeler gate-house for our club!"

"It's true, what Mart said," Honey said quietly. "It looked terrible, all choked with vines and so dilapidated. Daddy's so proud of the way we fixed it up without any help from anyone. That's one reason that he gave us the station wagon. He likes the things the Bob-Whites do."

"Trixie didn't give me half a chance to finish what I started to say— Oh, stand still a minute, can't you?" Mart said to Strawberry, who was pawing the ground, eager to get going. "I liked the work we did on the clubhouse. I was just trying to be a little bit funny. There's no end to the things Mr. Wheeler does to help our club—Di's dad, too, and our own mom and dad."

Honey shook her blond head. "There's more to it than that, Mart. When I think of the crazy, dressed-up kid I was before I met Trixie and the rest of you. . . . Heavens, I never even owned a pair of jeans before. I never had one day's fun in all my life till. . . ."

"Poor little rich girl!" Mart dried imaginary tears.

"It's true. Jim and I practically *live* at Crabapple Farm now . . . picnics and barbecues . . . your mother's cooking. It's a lot easier to give things to people when you have too much yourself. It's better to *do* things with and for other people. The Bob-Whites have taught us that, haven't they, Jim?"

"Sure! Of course, I'm a Johnny-come-lately—just since your family took pity on a down-and-out orphan, Honey, and adopted me. I sure think I fell into a great life with some great friends. It took a punk like that stepfather of mine to make me realize this."

"Ho-hum!" Mart broke in, pretending to stifle a yawn. "Is this a love-in, or are we going to ride?"

"Ride!" Trixie said briskly. "It doesn't hurt anyone, though, to stop now and then and think about good things people do. Too many people are running down our country and everyone in it, with a special hate for teen-agers. I like us. I like all of us." She turned Susie sharply, urged her into a trot, and called back over her shoulder, "You have to remember that Dan doesn't know about the car. Let's turn into the woods here."

They left Glen Road for a world of tangy spruce and pine as the intriguing shade of the trail closed around them.

Reddy and Patch spread out, barking deliriously as they caught the pungent scent of damp pine needles, spongy leaf mold, and elusive cottontails.

The surefooted horses picked their way, sniffing the fresh air, Jupiter snorting and shaking his black head, restive under Jim's tight control.

Ahead of them, at the edge of the clearing, they could see the rustic old cottage of Mr. Maypenny, the Wheeler gamekeeper. Nearby, Dan Mangan was cutting up a fallen tree.

When he heard the Bob-White whistle, he shouted a welcome they couldn't quite hear, but he grinned a greeting they couldn't mistake.

When they neared and called out the news, his grin broke into a whoop of joy.

"One-seventh of the car is yours," Mart added as he dismounted and dropped his reins to ground-tie Strawberry. "Jim and Brian will give you a driving lesson right away."

"How about that? A station wagon of our own!" Dan shouted to Mr. Maypenny, who had come out of his house when he heard Dan's whoop.

"It's no more than you all deserve," the game-keeper said. His eyes twinkled as Mart and Dan, irrepressible, went into an Indian war dance. It stopped abruptly, though, when Jupiter reared, exciting the gentler horses.

Mart raced to pick up Strawberry's reins, while the girls calmed their mounts.

The elderly man watched thoughtfully. Trixie wondered if he was thinking how miraculously Regan's rebellious nephew Dan had changed from a wild member of a tough New York City gang into the hardworking, happy lad he now was! It pleased her to think that the Bob-Whites had had something to do with that change.

"Dan, can we pick you up on the way back?" Jim called over his shoulder. "We're riding the horses into the woods for exercise."

"Go along with them," Mr. Maypenny told Dan. "Lay down the saw—the wood can wait—and saddle old Spartan. It'll do him good to get a little trail riding, too."

With a shout, Trixie held up her hand, fingers crossed. "I was hoping and wishing Dan could come!"

Dan rested his saw against the trunk of a tree and grinned his thanks to Mr. Maypenny. It didn't take him long to saddle Spartan and fall in behind the other Bob-Whites.

Single file, they rode on. Through heavy, overhanging branches they could glimpse the blue of the sky and feel the soft touch of late summer wind on their tanned faces.

Stirred by the sound of their voices and the yammering of the excited dogs, flocks of scolding birds rose. Little ground squirrels and cottontail rabbits skittered for refuge.

At the end of the woods trail, Jim, who was leading, held up his arm to signal the others to stop. From now on, the ground was barred to horses. Signs proclaimed this order.

The Bob-Whites tied their horses. Farther on, afoot, they came to other notices forbidding *any* further progress.

"I wish Dad owned this part between here and the bluff," Jim said. "He'd do more than warn

people. He'd fence off this part. He may do it yet, if
the county will let him."

Erosion had undermined the lip of the bluff so
that only a dangerously thin shelf remained, ready
to crumble and fall without warning.

Carefully the Bob-Whites circled the area till
they stood on higher and firmer ground. Here, in
a clump of pines, they would eat their sandwiches.

Beneath them the mighty Hudson flowed. Flat
ferries, heavy with beetle-sized cars, churned trails
that rocked tiny, white-sailed pleasure craft in their
wake. Gulls wheeled, dipping and soaring to the
tempo of tugboat whistles.

Immediately below the Bob-Whites lay their
objective: a strip of marshy land to be reached by
a worn and precipitous footpath. Swampy, of little
use to industry, it fascinated the young people. In
late fall it was a resting place for fowl on their
north-south flight. Even when the Beldens' grandfather had been a boy, botany classes from Sleepyside schools had hunted there to fill herbariums
with specimens.

Diana, shading her eyes to look far up the river,
walked, unthinking, into the forbidden area, only
to be jerked back by Jim with such force that she
sprawled on the ground.

"Can't you read?" he asked, fright hoarsening his
voice. "That shelf of earth is so thin that a rabbit's
whisper might break it off. Don't do that again,

Diana!" He helped her to her feet.

"That was a close call," Mart said seriously. "Girls! They have to be watched just like babies! Let's go back."

"We will not, Mart." Trixie's voice was impatient. "You're a fine one to talk! You'd have drowned half a dozen times in the Wheeler lake if a girl—Honey— hadn't pulled you out when you were learning to dive off the high board. And we're *not* going back till we see what those men down there are doing to the marsh."

"I'm sorry," Mart said, shamefaced. "When I get scared, I. . . . Let's go find out what's up."

Carefully they inched their way down, chain-fashion, hand in hand, loosening outcropping pebbles, and rejoicing in the thrill of this lesser danger.

Near the water's edge, men busy with sump pumps seemed to be drawing up samples of sand and vegetation for testing.

"What goes on?" Jim asked.

"Some outfit from Canada is going to build a factory here," one of the men said. "They're going to drain the swamp."

"That's been tried many times before," Jim said. The listening Bob-Whites nodded.

"It wouldn't work," Brian asserted. "There's no bottom to the marsh."

"They've found one now, kid," the man answered. "Some engineers came up with a new way of doing it. There's been enough publicity about the project. If you'd read the papers, you wouldn't have to ask so many questions and interrupt our work—you and a dozen others."

"Gosh! What'll we do for stuff for botany?" Mart wondered. "Where will the migrating birds light?"

"Questions! Questions! Questions!" the man snorted. "You'd better get out of our way . . . go back up to where you came from. Read the answers to your questions in the newspapers. Say," he added as they quickly crossed the road to the path, "aren't you going to take the old guy with you?"

Mart turned. "What old guy?"

"That old guy there. He asked more questions than you kids. Isn't he with you?"

Mart shook his head. "There's no old guy with us."

Trixie, though, had trained her keen eyes to hunt out details other people missed. She had to, to be a good detective.

Far up the road she saw a man fade into the shrubbery and out of sight.

A sense of something evil, something frightening, set her to shivering, though the day was warm and sunny.

A Mysterious Phone Call · 2

TRIXIE AND HONEY lingered, whispering, as the boys began the climb back up the path.

"You looked scared to death," Honey said under her breath. "What happened?"

"It was that man—the old man—didn't you see him?"

"No. I thought that workman was seeing things. Did you see someone?"

Trixie gave Honey a little shove to start her up the path. "Gleeps, if you'd only keep your eyes open! I was sure you saw him, too, and maybe could tell me who he was."

She had raised her voice, and Jim, trudging

ahead, overheard. "I saw him just as he disappeared, but, gosh, Trixie, he gave me a funny feeling—as if there were something I should know
about him."

"Forget the spooky guy," Brian said. "The only
thing that gives me the heebies is that I'm just in
the middle of a study of herbs. I've never found any
of them outside that marsh—tansy, boneset, berga-
mot, pennyroyal."

"I never even heard of them," Jim said.

"Not many people have today," Brian explained,
puffing as they neared the top. "They were used by
our great-grandmothers for medicine. I think
they're pretty neat today. I want to do some re-
search with them. I'll bet it's the only place in the
United States where you can find them still growing wild."

Jim laughed. "I'll take that bet. There's plenty
of marshland left, even here around Sleepyside.
If you keep on this way, Brian, you'll get your M.D.
before you even start premed."

"Then I can be the doctor in residence in your
home for orphan boys."

"I wish I had some sort of career to work toward
all the time," Diana sighed, her lovely face worried
and a little red from climbing. "Honey and Trixie
are so sure they want to be detectives. Mart's so
sure he wants to be a farmer, Brian a doctor, and
Dan a New York policeman. Jim has had his mind

set on that home for orphan boys ever since his great-uncle left him that money. I used to think I wanted to be a stewardess, but now I'm not sure I want to be anything—except a mother, maybe."

"We all want to be that," Honey was quick to say. "That's a career. Look at Trixie's mother. She mothers all of us. She's super!"

Trixie saw Honey's face sadden. Her own mother was away so much of the time on business trips with her father. There *was* Miss Trask, of course. She had been Honey's teacher at Briar Hall, before Honey came to Sleepyside and enrolled in public school. Now Miss Trask did a wonderful job as housekeeper at Manor House and of pinch-hitting as mother for Honey and Jim. All the Bob-Whites were devoted to her. She disciplined, but she didn't snoop. She listened but found little fault. Why, she made *almost* as good a mother as Trixie's own.

At the top of the cliff, Trixie and Honey stood looking back down below. The men were still busy dredging and sampling. Trixie's face clouded as the Bob-Whites started back to the horses and Manor House. That man—what was it about him that. . . .

"Stay with me tonight," Honey begged. "My mom is away, as usual, and we have so much to talk over."

"I shouldn't," Trixie said, hesitating. "I'm always

getting out of chores at home. Mom never says a
thing, but she does depend on me to watch Bobby.
He can get into more mischief."

"It won't be quite so much work for her if you
and Brian and Mart stay for dinner at our house.
Stay, please. Miss Trask will call your mother."

"And Moms will say yes. She never thinks about
herself. No, Honey, I have a better idea. Moms has
to get dinner for Bobby and Daddy, anyway. She
doesn't mind more people. You and Jim come to
dinner at our house. Before we left this morning,
Brian and Mart and I gathered the eggs and
brought in vegetables from the garden—tomatoes,
green beans, green cabbage, and some late lettuce.
If I run on home now and help, we'll have a sort of
picnic supper."

"I'll love it. So will Jim. But you'll have to
promise to stay with me tonight, anyway. Let me
go home with you now and help. I can at least read
to Bobby."

"And who, pray, will groom the horses?" Mart
asked.

"And clean the tack?" Jim added.

"I told the girls I'd help groom the horses if you
kids would exercise them," Regan said and took
Susie's and Lady's reins.

"That simplifies matters," Jim said. "Mart and
Brian and I will help Regan make short work of
things here at the stable. You girls help Mrs. Bel-

den. We'll drive our car after dinner. It's too bad Di and Dan went home, but we can call them."

"Perfect!" Trixie said. "We'll pick them up in the new Bob-White bus after dinner. Maybe we can all go to the movie in Sleepyside after we wash the dishes. Moms won't mind if we have dinner early, just as soon as Daddy gets home from the bank. We *did* agree to use Bob-White funds for a once-a-month movie, didn't we?"

"Right," Mart said. "And what better way to christen the new car? There's a western at the Cameo— Every once in a while my poor little sister comes up with an idea that's a bell ringer."

"Once in a while is better than never," Trixie retorted archly. Then they both laughed. They were so near the same age that they constantly baited one another. But let an outsider say anything critical about either one, and watch the fur fly!

The next morning Jim, Brian, and Mart had parked the station wagon in front of the Bob-White clubhouse. Jim was on his knees, painstakingly sketching the words BOB-WHITES OF THE GLEN, to be filled in later with bright red enamel, when Trixie came flying down the driveway from Manor House, followed by Honey.

"Jim," she shouted, *"who* is Betje Maasden?"

"Who's who? What?" Jim asked, startled, as Mart accidentally touched the horn.

"If Mart will keep still a minute, I'll explain. Someone called at your house just now. I answered the telephone, because nobody else seemed to be doing it. A gruff, mysterious voice asked for you."

"*Everything* is mysterious to Trixie," Mart said.

"Well, I keep thinking about that man I saw yesterday," Trixie answered, keeping her eyes on Jim.

"Of all the unmysterious things that could happen!" Mart gibed. "The poor guy was probably just curious. All you saw of him was his back, anyway."

"It was a mysterious back." Trixie shivered.

"I give up," Mart hooted. "Do I have a mysterious back, Mrs. Sherlock Holmes?" He struck a pose.

"You couldn't be mysterious if you tried," Trixie retorted. "You just talk too much. That man was sort of strange. Jim said he shivered, too, when he saw him."

"Jim would agree with you if you said you saw a dinosaur disappearing into the shrubbery. That doesn't prove anything."

"Let's get this show back on the road, Mart," Jim broke in. "What did you tell the man on the phone, Trix?"

"I said you weren't there—and could I take a message? He said yes, if I thought I had sense enough to remember it."

Jim bristled. "That was a great line to take. Just great. Then what?"

"Then he asked me if you ever had an aunt by the name of Betje Maasden. Did you?"

"Not that I ever heard of. The only relative I ever knew was my great-uncle, James Winthrop Frayne."

Mart whistled. "He was worth half a dozen other relatives, too. He left you Ten Acres."

"Which promptly burned to the ground," Trixie said.

"And," Mart went on pompously, "he left you half a million dollars. Nobody would sneeze at that kind of money."

"No," Brian said, "and Jim promptly salted it all away to build a school for runaway boys as soon as he's through college. I'm going to be his doctor."

"We all know that," Trixie said, somewhat impatiently. "Let's get back to Betje Maasden. The name somehow rings a bell. Didn't you *ever* have an Aunt Betje, Jim?"

"Nope," Jim answered. Then he sat up straight. "Say, wait a minute. My mother had an older sister —lots older. But she was Aunt Betty. I never saw her. Her maiden name was Vanderheiden, the same as my mother's."

" 'Betty' could be 'Betje,' " Honey said thoughtfully. "Lots of old Dutch names have turned into more modern ones."

"That's right," Jim said positively. "My own mother was Katje, but my father always called her

Katie. I never did hear the name Maasden, though,
as far as I can remember. Did you tell that guy off
who got so smart on the phone, Trixie?"

"No, I didn't. He slammed down the receiver
after he said he'd find out some other way—that he
had to know right away."

"You said the name Betje Maasden rang a bell
with you, Trixie. It does with me, too, sort of. Betje
Maasden, Betje Maasden." Jim's forehead wrinkled.

"I have it!" Trixie shouted triumphantly. "It's
the name that was in that story in the newspaper."

"What story? What newspaper?" Jim asked,
amused at Trixie's excitement.

"You know—the story Daddy read to us at dinner
last night when we told him about those men we
saw at the marsh. I guess nobody paid much attention. Our heads were so full of our new car. I'm
sure I remember the name Betje Maasden, though.
Where is the *Sleepyside Sun*? Is it up at your
house, Honey?"

"Now, it just happens—" Mart said, rolling up
his shirt sleeves and extending his hands as a
magician does. "See? Nothing up my sleeves!" He
reached in his hip pocket. "It just happens," he repeated, "that I have a copy of the little newspaper
with me. There's an advertisement in it that I
intend to bring up at our meeting, as soon as Trixie
forgets about Betje Maasden and gets down to
business."

"Read it first!" Trixie begged. "First read the story about the marsh, Mart. Please!"

"Okay. It has a local dateline.

> "The International Pine Company, of Montreal, Quebec, Canada, plans to build a million-dollar furniture factory in Sleepyside. It will offer employment to several hundred men and women.
>
> "The factory is to be built on the strip known as Blue Heron Marsh, just outside the city, along the Hudson River. Representatives of the Canadian company have been at work surveying the strip for reclamation.
>
> "The land is appraised at one hundred and fifty thousand dollars. Work will begin as soon as title to the land is established. The last name to appear on the abstract as owner of the land is Betje Maasden. No address is given. Research is under way now to locate Betje Maasden.

"Well, that's that!" Mart said and folded the newspaper. "Now let's get down to business."

"Oh, Mart," Trixie said, "can't you see this *is* business—that we have to find out who Betje Maasden is?"

"No, I don't see it, Trixie. I think it's none of your business or ours. However—" Mart gave a great sigh—"I might just as well resign myself to watching you and Honey go into action. The Belden-Wheeler Detective Agency is about to take over the Bob-Whites of the Glen again. I can see that."

"Have a heart, Mart," Brian said. "After all that excitement on the Mississippi River towboat, how do you think we can settle down to any routine? I'm for Trixie and Honey—and Betje, too. What's the next move, Trix?"

Trixie smiled gratefully. "Well, if anybody in this whole countryside knows anything about anyone called Maasden, it's sure to be Mrs. Vanderpoel. I suggest we pay her a visit."

Mrs. Vanderpoel had been a true friend to the Bob-Whites when they were planning their antique show for UNICEF. She had not only lent them many of her priceless antiques for use in the show, but she had also persuaded many of her friends among the old Dutch families to do so.

Since Crabapple Farm was only a short distance from the quaint yellow brick home where Mrs. Vanderpoel's family had lived for generations, Brian, Mart, Trixie, and Bobby visited her often. She liked them and they liked her. Fat, jolly, gray-haired, and hospitable, she had a bottomless jar filled with spicy Dutch windmill cookies, kept just for the Beldens and their friends in the Bob-White club.

"Before I can go anyplace or do anything, I have to go home and help Moms," Trixie said. "I was gone yesterday and last night, and—jeepers, I just remembered! Moms has to go to the dentist this morning, and I promised to take care of Bobby. If he's turned loose alone in the house, he'll tear everything apart to see what makes it work."

"Psychiatrists say that children must be encouraged to find out things for themselves," Mart said. "They don't know Bobby."

"I'll say they don't," Brian agreed. "Last week he opened my butterfly collection and put all the specimens out on the porch 'to see if they'd fly.' They were broken to pieces, of course, and no good after that. You'd better get home right away, Trix, before Moms gets away and the little fixer is turned loose."

"How about you and Mart coming home with me? It seems to me Dad had his 'now or else' voice last night when he talked about cutting the lawn."

"I'll help," Jim said quickly, "as soon as I finish this lettering on the station wagon. If we're going to get our weekly allowances and chip in on the Bob-White club fund, we'll all have to get to work, I guess. The fund sure looked sick after we shelled out for the movie last night."

Honey put her hand over her mouth. "I just remembered. Last night I brought all that mending home to do for your mother and then forgot all about it. I can't expect her to pay me if I don't keep it up. Buttons, buttons, buttons! Sometimes I think Bobby pulls them off just to keep me busy. Well, if he didn't, I wouldn't get a chance to do mending, and it's the first money I ever earned in my life."

"It's not a bad rule we made about club funds—that we have to earn the money we put up," Mart

said. "Let's get going and get the lawn mowed.
Then we can go sleuthing with Trixie. I want to
hear, myself, what Mrs. Vanderpoel has to say
about this Betje what's-her-name."

"How about taking the horses?" Jim suggested.
"Mrs. Vanderpoel's house is back in the woods, you
know, and Regan will be wanting us to exercise the
horses if he knows we're going."

"I'll call Di," Honey said. "Then I'll see you later.
She can ride Sunny down to your house, and we'll
put her to work, too."

The Faded Snapshot • 3

AT CRABAPPLE FARM, Mrs. Belden was just leaving when Trixie and the boys arrived.

"Heavens, I'm glad to see you," she said. "I didn't know where you were, and I was going to have to take Bobby with me to the dentist. I know how Dr. Morrison would like that!"

Trixie laughed. "The last time he was there, he tried to make a deal with Dr. Morrison, didn't he? Bobby wanted him to save all the teeth he pulled, so he could put them under his own pillow and collect for them from the Tooth Fairy."

"Say, that's a good deal!" Mart said and ruffled Bobby's hair. "I wish I'd thought it up."

"You thought up plenty at his age," his mother reminded him. "Trixie, I had to leave the breakfast dishes for you to do; then there's the dusting. And, boys, how about the lawn? I'd advise you to finish it before your father comes home from the bank."

"We're on our way, Moms." Mart went to get the can of gasoline for the mower. Then he called through the screen door, "When your slaves get all this work done, they're going to ride over to Mrs. Vanderpoel's house. Is that okay? Moms, don't race the motor when you start the car. You'll scare Strawberry and Susie and Lady."

"I learned to drive before you were born," his mother called. "And I learned to ride and not to scare horses long before Brian was born. It's all right for you to go to Mrs. Vanderpoel's house, but you'll have to take Bobby."

Bobby clapped his hands. "I'll go to see Old Brom while you're at Mrs. Vanderpoel's, Trixie, so you can quit frownin'. I'd rather go there, anyway. Course, I'll stop long enough to get some cookies at Mrs. Vanderpoel's house."

"I can count on that, all right," Trixie said as she tied a coverall apron around her waist and ran hot water into the sink. "I *wish* we had a dishwasher!"

"Moms thinks she has—you!" Brian said and dodged out the door to escape a shower of soapy water. "Gosh, here comes Di now, and she has her little twin brothers riding up in front of her. What chance do we have with *three* monsters?"

"Larry and Terry can come with me to visit Old Brom," Bobby said, jumping from one foot to another. "He'll tell us some whoppers. Remember the one he told us about No-mah-ka-ta, the witch who lives on top of the highest Catskill? You know, that first time I ever met him."

"I sure do remember," Trixie said, smiling. "Every time it's rained since that time, you tell us it's the old witch spinning clouds and sending the winds racing to the four corners of the earth."

"Well, I like Old Brom. He's my friend."

"You're right. He doesn't seem to want many friends—just you and Mrs. Vanderpoel. He's a hermit. He'd rather be alone. He won't be alone today, with you three young hoodl—"

"He likes boys—little boys—'cause they don't interr...."

"Interrupt."

"That's right. Today maybe he'll tell us about *The Flying Dutchman*. Do you s'pose he piloted a jet?"

Jim arrived in time to hear Bobby's question.

"Not a chance, fella," he told the little boy. "They only had sailing ships in those days. Captain Marryat told us about *The Flying Dutchman* in his book *The Phantom Ship*. See if Trix will read it to you."

"Will you, Trixie?" Bobby asked. "Hi, Terry! Hi,

Larry! We're going to Old Brom's house!"

Trixie sent the little boys out in the yard to play
till the Bob-Whites were ready to leave. With the
help of Diana and Honey, she made quick work
of the dusting and dishes.

Under Mart's guidance, the power mower
zoomed around the large lawn. Brian followed with
the clippers and Jim with the broom. It wasn't long
till everything was shipshape, inside and out, and
they were off for the brick house in the woods.

Each big boy took a little boy in front of him
on his saddle. They entered the woods far down
Glen Road, for the brick cottage was just on the
fringe of the game preserve.

When they knocked at her door, Mrs. Vanderpoel turned from the oven of the old-fashioned
stove which filled a corner of her kitchen.

"I just knew I'd be having visitors," she said,
pushing her gray curls back from her plump, heat-
reddened face. "I never was so glad to see anyone.
And the little boys, too!" She lifted a corner of her
blue checked apron and wiped the perspiration
from her chin. "Bobby, could you boys eat a nice,
warm windmill cookie?"

"Yes, ma'am! We're going to call on Old Brom."

"Now, that will really please him. You can take
him some fresh cookies, too."

"If he can find his mouth behind his bushy whiskers," Bobby said, giggling, his mouth full of

crumbled cookie. "Wait till you see those whiskers!" he told the Lynch twins. "They're just like Rip Van Winkle's. Is this the bag for Old Brom?"

Without waiting for an answer, he scooped up a handful of cookies, shouted his thanks, and disappeared down the footpath, with the Lynch boys scurrying to keep up.

"Well, now, that's that!" Mrs. Vanderpoel said. "If you'll bring the jug of cool milk out of the well house, Trixie, we can all sit down here at the table. Where's Dan?"

"He couldn't come with us today. Mr. Maypenny had work that had to be done right away. Anyway, this is a business call, Mrs. Vanderpoel," Trixie explained. "Mmmm, this milk is good."

"Did you fill all the mugs?" Mrs. Vanderpoel asked anxiously and peered around. "That's right!" She heaped the cookie plate again, then settled into the big captain's chair at the head of the table. She blew on her glasses, wiped them clear with her apron, then asked, "Business you say, Trixie? A business call?"

"Yes. You know everyone who has ever lived around Sleepyside, Mrs. Vanderpoel, particularly the old Dutch families. Did you ever hear the name Betje Maasden?"

Mrs. Vanderpoel thought. "I've known several Betjes. There was Betje Van Bronck, Betje Schimmel, Betje— Why, Jim, your own mother's sister was Betje—Betje Vanderheiden! Seems to me I remember she went to Holland to live when she married. That was a long time ago, Jim. She married a big blond giant of a man . . . Wilhelm . . . Wilhelm. . . . I can't remember his last name."

"Was it Maasden?" Trixie asked anxiously.

"I don't think so. I don't know. Let me see. . . . I should remember; I saw a picture of her not long ago."

"Can you remember where?" Trixie prodded.

Mrs. Vanderpoel closed her eyes, thinking. "It wasn't in an album. I remember holding it in my hand. . . ."

"In that tin box, maybe?" Trixie asked, jumping to her feet in her excitement. "The one you have in your desk?"

"Maybe if you'd give her a chance to think, Trixie, instead of dancing around her and making her nervous . . ." Mart suggested.

"I'm sorry," Trixie said, then added, "Is it in that box, maybe, Mrs. Vanderpoel?"

She couldn't understand why everyone, even Mrs. Vanderpoel, laughed.

"Take it easy, Trix!" Mart chuckled. "You're as nervous as a cat."

"Never mind, child," Mrs. Vanderpoel said kindly, "I'm not at all sure it's in the tin box in my desk, but bring it to me, and we'll see."

Trixie brought the box. Then, with superhuman

control, she sat quietly across the table from the kindly Dutch woman and watched as she took out the old Kodak pictures, looked at each one carefully, and set it aside.

Some of them almost brought tears, and Mrs. Vanderpoel apologized. "I don't know why I hold on to all these old pictures. They always make me sad. Oh, well, some of them make me glad, too, and that evens everything up. Here we are, Jim! Your Aunt Betje and her husband and their little girl."

She passed the faded picture across to Jim, and Trixie, looking over his shoulder, asked quickly, "Where are they now?"

"Yes, Mrs. Vanderpoel," Jim asked soberly, "and why didn't you ever show me this picture before? I thought I hadn't a relative in the world."

"You haven't, Jim." Mrs. Vanderpoel's voice was sad. "That's why I never showed you the picture before. A very tragic thing happened to all of them. The automobile in which they were riding went off the road and into a canal. They were drowned."

No one said a word. Even Trixie was silenced. She just sat, holding the picture in her hand, turning it this way and that.

"There's something written on the back," Honey said, breaking the silence.

Trixie turned the little picture over, then handed it to Jim.

"Betje and Wilhelm Maasden," Jim read, "and Juliana. Sixteen Seestrasse, The Hague."

"There's your Betje Maasden," Jim said quietly to Trixie. "And I never saw her in all my life."

"It happened so many years ago," Mrs. Vanderpoel reminded him. "All of fifteen years, I'd say. It's too bad the date of the picture isn't written on the back. People should always record the date. If I'm not being too curious, why all this interest in someone called Betje?"

Then they told her of the marshland, of the story in the newspaper, of the title to the land, and of the search being made to find Betje Maasden.

"It's a wonder nobody thought of asking me before this," Mrs. Vanderpoel said. "Someone from the library calls me about once a month to ask about old families in this part of Westchester County. There wasn't any other kin to Betje Maasden but your mother, Jim. I guess, since she's gone and your Aunt Betje is gone, that means the land properly belongs in your name."

"I guess so," Jim answered, shaking his head sadly. "For a while I hoped maybe you'd turned up someone related to me."

Honey, sitting on the other side of Jim, put her hand on her adopted brother's arm to comfort him.

He smiled at her and said, "I guess that's that."

"Except that you'll have to have some more information for the office of deeds at the courthouse,"

Brian said. "Don't forget that strip of land is valued at one hundred and fifty thousand dollars. It seems as though it will be yours, Jim."

"If it is, it'll go for a special dormitory for my orphan boys, and I'll call it—"

"The Betje Maasden Dormitory!" Trixie cried excitedly. "We'd better take this picture to the courthouse in Sleepyside."

"They'll want to write a letter to The Hague and try to get some more information about the Maasden family," Brian said.

"I'll write, too," Trixie said, "just as soon as we collect the little boys and take the horses back to the stable."

"For pete's sake, why do you think *you* have to write a letter?" Mart asked. "I'd say your detective parade went up an alley this time. You'll have to find another mystery, Trix, you and Honey."

"Oh, no, I won't," Trixie said—with a smile that Mart knew only too well. "I'm going to write a letter to The Hague myself, because I know Jim wants as much information as he can get, don't you, Jim?"

"Yes, and it's good of you to do it, Trixie. I'm no good at writing to strangers. I just hope there's someone who knew my aunt and uncle and cousin. It *was* a long time ago."

"You didn't have that Cheshire cat look on your face just because you were going to write a letter," Mart told Trixie. "I mean the look you had when I told you 'no more mystery.'"

"No, I didn't, Mart Belden," Trixie said firmly.
"You haven't forgotten that mysterious voice that
asked about Betje Maasden over the telephone.
And you haven't forgotten that mysterious man
who was asking questions when we were down at
the marsh, have you, hmmm?"

"Oh, no!" Mart said and hid his face in his arms
in mock agony. "I should have known. I should
have known!"

Practice for the Turf Show • 4

WHEN THE BOB-WHITES took the picture of Betje Maasden to the courthouse, the man in the office of deeds promised Trixie he would get a letter of inquiry off to Holland the next morning. Her own letter to The Hague also was mailed the next morning. Then the waiting period began for the impatient Trixie.

Routine activity helped—work at the hospital with other Candy Stripers and helping with late-summer canning at home. There was swimming, too, in the big Wheeler lake, and tennis, riding, exercising the horses, and jumping, in preparation for the Turf Show. How Trixie loved the little black mare Susie!

Regan had been more than ordinarily demanding about the Turf Show coming up in the fall. He wanted the Bob-Whites to be perfectly trained for every event they entered. He knew his horses had a fine chance of winning in the conformation competition and various walking contests. It was jumping that concerned him most. It took constant practice. So, when he found the Bob-Whites with a day free just for jumping practice, he was glad.

"Some of you can use a lot of polishing," he told the Bob-Whites assembled around him at the Wheeler stable.

"He looked right at me," Trixie whispered to Honey. "I don't really blame him. I've had so many things on my mind, I haven't had time to try to jump. It's a wonder he hasn't been after me before this. Heavens, do you realize we have a booth to get ready for that show, too—all those handmade articles to be sold?"

"We still have plenty of time to work on the booth. It's the show itself—riding—that's the most important thing."

"I know that, and I'll never be the jumper you are, no matter how I try. It scares me."

"It's the only thing I've ever known that frightened you," Jim said, laughing. "If you lived at Manor House, you'd soon jump over the moon.

Regan sure keeps after Honey and me. You haven't done so badly on Susie, Trixie. Jupiter really takes tight handling. Hey—don't you know any better than that?"

Trixie had crossed back of the big black gelding and he had kicked out at her, startling her out of her wits.

"I know, I know," she said, her voice shaking. "I shouldn't have walked back of him—just around him—and I should have kept talking to him all the time. I've heard Regan often enough on the subject. I'm glad Susie isn't so temperamental."

"Any startled horse will kick—even gentle Susie; remember that, Trixie," Regan said tersely.

"Just so you don't start the day off mad at me, Regan," Trixie answered meekly. "Jupiter's such a big show-off."

"I hope he shows off at the Turf Club next month," Jim said. "Don't forget that Dad took a blue with him this summer at the International Show."

The stable was large, neat, and comfortable, and fragrant with well-soaped leather and good hay. Regan was justly proud of it and proud of the ribbons and the posted record of horse-handling. He would have liked it if the Wheeler horses could have entered every show in a four-county area around Sleepyside. He realized, however, that Mr. Wheeler's first interest was in recreation for his

son and daughter and their friends. When they did
compete, though, Regan wanted them to reflect
credit on his training.

"Here comes Dan now," Mart said, "with Di. I
wonder what they're laughing about."

"Do you know what Dan just told me?" Diana
said a few minutes later as she reined in Sunny and
slid out of the saddle. "You'd never guess in a hundred years. He said Spartan can *dance!*"

"He *can*," Dan insisted to the hooting Bob-
Whites. "The man Mr. Wheeler bought him from
said he used to be in a circus. I forgot about that
till this morning. I had to get up real early to look
over some traps for Mr. Maypenny. I took my transistor along—"

"And went to sleep and dreamed Spartan was
dancing," Mart broke in.

Dan just ignored him. "I had the 'Whispering
Strings' on. You know that trio that's playing at the
hotel in White Plains? Well, I was just riding along
listening. All at once I noticed that Spartan was
doing some fancy wriggling. I thought maybe he'd
stepped in a rabbit hole, but it wasn't that. He was
waltzing! He threw out his left back leg, then
picked up his front right and—"

"Waltzing!" Trixie cried. "*Spartan?*"

"Yeah . . . three-quarter time!" Dan said and
patted Spartan's shoulder. "Want to see him do it?"

"This is one I've got to see," Regan said.

"I brought my radio with me. Watch. I'll turn it on." Dan dialed for the music. "Spartan's a real ham," he added proudly. "Watch him!"

The handsome old roan really did dance, awkwardly and a little shakily but unmistakably in time to the music. He didn't even seem to mind when the Bob-Whites took up the rhythm and clapped out the beat. He just danced faster.

Regan pushed his cap back on his head. "Now I've seen everything. Say, this gives me an idea. We can dress Spartan up and use him for the clown at the horse show—" He broke off at sight of Dan's frowning face.

Dan jumped off the old horse, backed him up, and turned him around to face the group. "Spartan's no clown!" he said in a resentful tone. "He's smarter than any other horse around here. Just because he's old and maybe not a Thoroughbred—"

"Oh, come off it," Regan told his nephew. "Nobody's running down your horse. There's Arabian blood in him, too, Dan, even if it is tired blood after twenty-five years. He has more Arabian blood than any of these other horses, except Susie."

Dan perked up, but he still thrust out his lip. "He's no clown, anyway."

"What's wrong with being the clown?" Mart asked.

"Yeah," Brian added. "The clown horse is always the hit of the whole show. Any well-trained horse can go through all the paces: walking, trotting, galloping, cantering, even jumping. It takes a real star to clown."

"Brian's right," Honey said. "But Spartan doesn't have to be a clown to do his dance. He would look cute, though, dressed up. . . ."

"With a tutu around his tummy," Trixie added excitedly, "and a wreath of flowers on his head."

"Spartan's no *girl* horse, Trixie," Dan said and kicked the gravel in disgust. "I'd rather he'd be the clown than that. He does kinda like the limelight, and if you think it would add to the show. . . ."

"It'll *make* the show." Regan's face lit up. "Will you do it, Dan?"

Dan nodded. "If Spartan will."

"Then let's get on with the jumping," Regan said. "Trixie, bring Susie in from the pasture and saddle her. Jupiter's the only horse I kept in the stable this morning. Jim will have to let him run for a while before he saddles him. He's too high-spirited right now."

Humming "The Blue Danube," Dan tied Spartan in one of the stalls and went out to the pasture to help Regan set up the jumps.

The other Bob-Whites scattered. Diana intended only to watch the practice, because Sunny was not a jumper. There were only three other palominos in the county, and all they would do in the show would be to march and look beautiful.

Trixie climbed over the pasture fence and snapped her fingers to call Susie. The little black mare cantered over to take the carrot Trixie held out to her. When she had crunched it juicily, she sniffed at the pocket where it had been hidden and bumped Trixie lovingly with her nose, wanting more.

Something deep within Trixie stirred as she ran her hand lovingly down Susie's neck and put her face close to the little mare's cheek.

She had always longed for a horse of her very own, and Susie was the nearest thing to it. She told Susie secrets she didn't even tell Honey.

As she led the mare into the stable to saddle her, Trixie talked to Susie about Spartan's dancing and the upcoming show and the need for practice.

The little mare nodded her head up and down, as though she understood every word. Trixie was sure she did, and would have gone on to tell her about the marsh and Betje Maasden, except that suddenly they were inside the stable. Here the other Bob-Whites were laughing, talking, and saddling their horses.

Trixie took the tack from the peg in the room where it hung just so. Regan was strict about this— stirrups on the leathers, girth thrown over the saddle, bridle on the hook right under the saddle peg. No Bob-White would have thought of putting gear back any other way.

Absentmindedly Trixie saddled Susie, walked her a little, tightened the girth, mounted, then, along with Honey, trotted through the pasture gate.

"You're having one of your faraway days," Honey said. "I'm just as interested in that strip of land and its owner as you are—more so, maybe, because it's my brother Jim's aunt. Right now, though, we'd better concentrate on our jumping. We owe something to Regan for the way he looks after us and our horses, you know—to say nothing of his baby-sitting Bobby when we need some privacy."

Trixie grasped Susie's reins more tightly and smiled at Honey. "You're right. You always are. I wish I didn't have such a one-track mind. But this will take so much time. Maybe I should ask Regan to let me help with some of the paper work for the show instead of jumping."

Honey sat up straight on Lady, and Trixie slowed, startled by the look on Honey's face.

"Trixie Belden, just try putting your one-track mind on practicing. Sometimes you make me furious. Sometimes I think I don't even want to be a detective!"

"Don't say that!" Trixie said, stunned. "It's our life work. Jumping isn't."

"Try to act as though it is, at least today," Honey begged. "The show means so much to Regan."

"I know that, and I do want to do my best. But

if we ride in the Turf Show, it'll mean daily practice for the next six weeks. I won't have a chance to do anything else. I *have* to do my work at the hospital. I *have* to help Moms. What I want to do more than anything in the world is to try to solve mysteries. We're just at the beginning of a good one now—Betje Maasden and that man at the marsh."

"Oh, Trixie, they haven't anything to do with one another," Honey said, laughing. "Anyway, the Turf Show won't require daily practice. Regan said once a week, if we practice hard. And I'll help you with the housework and Bobby too."

All morning, out in the pasture, Trixie watched Jupiter sail proudly over the bars and watched Brian on Starlight and Mart on Strawberry take their turns.

It looked so easy, even for Honey on Lady. But, somehow, even though Trixie brought Susie right up to the bar at a romping gallop, the little horse turned her head and just walked around it.

"I'll never be able to jump," Trixie told Regan, almost in tears.

"That's right," he agreed. "You never will and Susie never will, unless you keep your mind on what you are doing. Susie can take those jumps without half trying. The trouble is with you. Try it again. This time put your heart into it. If you throw your heart and your mind into the effort, you and the horse will jump together."

"We'll try it, Regan," Trixie said, ashamed. "This time I think we're going to make it."

When her turn came, Trixie circled the jumps several times, talking to Susie, petting her, and encouraging her. Then, confidently, she headed for the first hurdle, rose lightly over Susie's withers, and gave the takeoff signal.

Up they soared—and over!

A cry went up from the other Bob-Whites, who had watched, without comment, Trixie's many attempts and failures.

"Susie never touched the bar with her hooves!" Trixie called triumphantly. "May I try it again, Regan, even if it's out of turn?"

"Go ahead," Regan said. "Good girl! Keep at it while the going's good!"

When she slowed at the end of four jumps, Trixie turned Susie and cantered up to where Regan was standing.

"That was real show riding," he told her. "Nothing to it, is there, Trixie?"

Trixie slid out of her saddle and put her head close to Susie's. "When I'm riding Susie, there isn't!"

Back in the stable, Trixie rubbed, currycombed, and brushed Susie till the small mare nickered her gratitude for being made so comfortable.

Trixie gave her a final pat. "As soon as you cool off a little, I'll feed you and give you fresh water."

Jupiter, still restive, even after the strenuous

morning, had to be crosstied before Jim could approach him with the currycomb. He had been superb. There wasn't a horse to match him in all of Westchester County. Nevertheless, Trixie gave him a wide berth as she walked around the stable to join Honey.

The two girls sat side by side, soaping and rubbing leather and shining chrome till it sparkled. Then all the Bob-Whites hung up their tack exactly right, for Regan was watching out of the corner of his eye.

"It seems to me," Dan said as he measured out the horses' feed for his uncle, "that you don't need to talk about jumping *quite* so loud around Spartan. Horses have feelings. Suppose you'd been a prize pitcher for the Mets, and then you got to be as old as thirty, maybe, and had to listen to a lot of guff about a new record for strikeouts. How would you feel?"

"Do you mean Spartan used to be a jumper?" Mart asked.

"I'll say he was. Ask my uncle."

"Was he, Regan?"

"The best. Look at those legs. Look at that chest and shoulders! He jumped in the circus. He was one of the Cossack horses, too. He grew old in the business. Mr. Wheeler bought him for Dan to use for light work in helping Mr. Maypenny."

"He has a good life now," Dan said as he untied

Spartan and backed him out of the stall. "But he's like an elephant. He remembers way back when. Look at that gleam in his eye!"

Spartan seemed to know he was being discussed. He perked up his head, wriggled his big body, and pawed the ground.

Dan laughed and led him out to where Diana was waiting with Sunny. "See you later!" he called as they rode off.

"What a day!" Regan went about straightening this, hanging up that, running his hand down each horse's withers to see if they were cool enough to be watered. "Great jumping you did today!"

The Bob-Whites glowed.

"Even me?" Trixie asked.

"Yep, Miss Fidget, even you," Regan said, "at last."

Juliana Is Alive! • 5

EVERY MORNING Trixie was the first person to reach the postbox on Glen Road after the postman had passed. Every morning she came back looking woebegone.

"You seem to think Holland isn't any farther away than White Plains," Mart told her. "Give the transcontinental mail a chance. Maybe there isn't any such address now as Sixteen Seestrasse in The Hague. Time marches on, you know."

"I thought about that, smarty, and addressed the letter to occupant or neighbor. Oh, Mart, why do you always have to keep finding fault with me?"

"Me? Finding fault with you? That's a laugh.

Did you hear that, Moms? Who's always telling me, 'Mart, feed the chickens; Mart, bring in the ripe tomatoes; Mart, do this; Mart, do that,' hmmm? I ask you, who?"

"Maybe I ask you to do all those things, but you never do them, does he, Moms?"

"Is that so? Where did those eggs over there in that basket come from? Where did those tomatoes come from?"

"I brought them in, not you. Moms is going to make catsup. I have the water boiling to loosen the skins so I can peel them for her. What are you going to do?"

Mrs. Belden reached for a box of spice high on a kitchen shelf and measured some into the kettle on the stove. "Mart is going to pick some green peppers and onions and bring them to me," she said. "But first, both of you are going to stop complaining about one another. I have more work to do today than seven women. Why does all the garden stuff ripen at once? Trixie, where is Bobby? He was bouncing a ball in here not more than three minutes ago."

"Here I am, Moms!" Bobby called as he burst through the door. "And I've got Trixie's letter with a funny stamp on it. Here, Trixie." He thrust it into her hand. "What does it say?"

"Give me time to open it," Trixie said, slitting the envelope. "Down, Reddy! It isn't for you."

Bobby put his arm around the dog's neck to quiet him. "He wants to know what it says, the same as us. What *does* it say, Trixie?"

"Jeepers! It's a long one. Here, Moms, you take it and read it out loud. I'm too excited. Brian!" she called through the door to her elder brother who was clipping the grass. "Come and hear the letter from Holland! There, now, Moms. Begin."

"You'd think it was a letter from the President of the United States," Mrs. Belden said, laughing. She turned the flame low under the boiling kettle. "Here goes. It's headed 'The Hague, *eighteen* Seestrasse.'"

"A neighbor did get it; see, Mart?" Trixie gloated.

"All right. All right. Just let Moms read it," Mart countered.

Brian waited, clippers in hand. "I sure second the motion, Trixie."

Trixie just glared at both boys and settled herself to listen.

"'Dear Miss Belden:'"

She only got that far when Bobby collapsed, giggling.

"What *is* the matter with you?" Trixie asked impatiently.

"*Miss* Belden. *Miss* Belden. Only teachers are 'Miss.' Trixie's not a 'Miss.'" A giggle caught in his throat, and he spluttered, choking.

"I'll try again," Mrs. Belden said. This time she skipped the "Miss Belden." She knew Bobby.

"Your letter came as a surprise to me but a welcome one. After all these years, there is now word from the family of my friend Betje Maasden. I had not known there was any relative of Betje's still living. We had heard that her sister married again and died in some eastern city in your country.

"It is true, tragically, that my friend and her husband were drowned when their automobile fell into the canal.

"It is not true, however, that their daughter, Juliana, was drowned. She was saved. Since there seemed to be no living relative, I took Juliana into my home, and we have loved her dearly. My own two children were grown, and it made me happy to have a young child in the family again. Ample funds were left in trust for Juliana by her father. She was sent to a private school here.

"Eight years ago my daughter, Mrs. Walter De Jong, and her husband moved to the United States, where he is in charge of his company's American office. They now live in the Bronx. My daughter and I thought Juliana might have greater educational advantages in the States, so she went with them and is now in your country, where she attended college. She is engaged to be married to a young attorney in The Hague.

"Juliana will be so happy to have the news, which I shall write to her, that she has a young cousin, James Winthrop Frayne. You will be getting in touch with one another soon, I am sure, and both you and Juliana will write to me of this happy occasion."

The letter was signed "Minna Schimmel."

"Whoopee!" Trixie cried. "The Bronx isn't far from here. Why didn't she give the DeJong family's address?"

"What difference does it make? We can look it up in a directory, I suppose," Mart said. "Where are you going?"

"To tell Jim, of course. May we possibly be excused, Moms? Brian and Mart and me? This calls for a Bob-White emergency meeting. Please, Moms! I'll work even harder than ever after the meeting."

"I know better than to try and stop you, Trixie. Go ahead, all of you. I'll call Honey and tell her to meet you at the clubhouse. She can call Diana and Dan."

"Oh, Moms, you're the greatest!"

"I'll go, too," Bobby said. "I want to know what you do."

"Oh, I'm sorry," Trixie said. "Meetings are for Bob-Whites only, Bobby. In a few years you can be a Bob-White yourself."

Bobby's lip trembled. "I'm the one who brought you the letter. . . ."

"Who'll taste the catsup for me, so I'll know when it's just right?" his mother asked.

"Let Reddy taste it. Let me go, Trixie!"

Mrs. Belden steered Bobby to a low kitchen chair near the stove, where the catsup was cooking.

"You stay with me, Bobby, because I don't want to stay alone. After they're all gone, I'll tell you where I've hidden a brand-new jigsaw puzzle."

"All right . . . but I never get to go anywhere! I can telephone Honey," he told his mother. "I know her number."

When all the members reached the clubhouse, Trixie opened the letter and read it dramatically. "Isn't it exciting? A cousin you never knew you had, Jim."

"Yeah," he said slowly and reached for the letter. "I like to think I still have at least one living relative."

Honey gasped. "Oh, Jim! You know that since Daddy and Mother adopted you, all of our relatives are your relatives, too."

"I know," Jim said quickly, "and you've all sure been wonderful to me. But it isn't *quite* the same as blood relatives."

"How about that stepfather of yours?" Mart asked, mostly to see what Trixie would say.

He found out.

"Mart Belden, don't you ever mention that cruel, mean stepfather of Jim's again. No wonder Jim doesn't think of him as family. He wasn't a *blood* relative, anyway."

"I can't bear to think of how terribly he treated you," Honey said and put her hand on her brother's arm. "He beat you and starved you and even tried to burn you in that old house! It's terrible! Thank goodness he's no longer your guardian. We've heard the last of him."

"I *hope* we have," Trixie said devoutly, a far-away look in her eyes.

"Let's forget about that and think about Juli-ana!" Honey said firmly.

"She's lots older than us," Diana said, "if she's old enough to have gone to college and to be engaged! Imagine that!"

"Maybe she won't even like to do the same things we do," Dan said. "Do you think so, Mart?"

"She'll like her handsome cousin," Mart answered and grinned as he saw Jim's freckled face color. "Furthermore," Mart said and touched his waistline, "even someone with a beard down to here would like to ride a horse."

"And ride in the Bob-White station wagon!" Diana said.

"And go swimming!" Brian added. "And go picnicking in the woods and everything!"

Jim took up the letter and read it again, folded it, and gave it back to Trixie. His face was serious. "Even if she *is* older, we'll get along fine. I'm sure to like her, because she's my mother's niece. I *wish* my mother could have lived." His eyes brightened as he looked at Trixie. "She was a lot like your mom."

Trixie's face saddened. Everyone couldn't have

a mother like Moms. Of course, Jim's adopted
mother, Mrs. Wheeler, like her husband, gave
Honey and Jim every material thing they wanted.

She watched Honey's face. It reflected loyalty
and love for her mother. Trixie knew, though, that
Honey realized what Jim meant when he said his
own mother had been like Moms. She was always
right there when she was needed. Mrs. Wheeler
was beautiful and kind— Oh, well, Moms was
Moms, and Mrs. Wheeler was Mrs. Wheeler.

Mrs. Minna Schimmel had said in her letter that
her family loved Juliana. The Bob-Whites would
love her, too, if only because she was Jim's cousin.

"Let's go up to the house," Honey said impul-
sively, "and call Juliana."

"That's an idea," Jim agreed. "We can ask her to
come right over here to our house."

"Tell her we'll meet her at the bus station," Mart
said.

At the Wheeler house thay all gathered around
Trixie as she began leafing through the telephone
directory. "Here's her number. Walter De Jong; it's
seven digits. Everyone quiet!"

Jim dialed and listened to the ring.

Nobody answered.

He waited a little, then dialed again—and again
—and again.

A big sigh went up from the Bob-Whites sitting
on the floor around the telephone. What a letdown,

after the excitement of the letter!

"I was *sure* she'd answer," Trixie said. "Wouldn't you think she'd stay home or even telephone you, Jim, after she got Mrs. Schimmel's letter?"

"Oh, Trixie, pipe down," Mart said.

"She probably left home before the postman came," Brian said. "Or maybe Mrs. Schimmel mailed a letter to her after she mailed the one to you."

"Or probably she went to have her hair washed and ironed and her eyelashes replaced," Mart added.

Trixie gave him a scornful look. "Now it's your turn to pipe down, Mart."

"I'll try again later," said Jim, "and keep on trying. In the meantime, why don't we surprise Regan and take out the horses?"

"Not the Beldens," Trixie said quickly, before Mart and Brian had a chance to say yes. "It's back to the mines for us. Brian's cutting the grass, and Mart and I have to help Moms. She's making catsup. Whistle for us if you get in touch with Juliana. If you ride, Honey, do be careful when you go near that ledge above the marsh!"

"As if Jim would let me go within a mile of it!" Honey laughed. "Remember how he yanked Di back when she wandered toward it?"

Trixie and her brothers worked hard all afternoon, and the big Belden kitchen was fragrant with the spicy smell of freshly bottled catsup.

At dinner Mr. Belden read the letter from Holland. "There's a news story in the *Sleepyside Sun* tonight with much the same information," he said. "It quotes a letter received at the courthouse from Mrs. Schimmel. This should put an end to all the phony claims for that strip of land. It will belong to Juliana. What did Jim have to say about a new cousin?"

"Gol, he went wild!" Mart said. "He tried to telephone her this morning. We found the De Jong number in the telephone book. Nobody answered."

"I guess nobody has answered yet, or we'd have heard from Jim or Honey," Trixie said. "I wonder what she'll be like . . . Jim's cousin!"

The next morning, while Trixie was bustling around helping her mother get breakfast, the call came from Jim.

When she had replaced the receiver, Trixie said to her mother, "Jim still hasn't been able to get Juliana on the phone. He and Honey want to drive over there. They want Brian and Mart and me to go, too. He wants us all to wear our Bob-White jackets Honey made for us. May we go, Moms?"

"Of course. I'm going to take things easy, after all that work with the catsup yesterday. Bobby and I are going to pick up the Lynch twins and drive to White Plains to get a new tire for his bike. I think it's a good idea for all of you to go over to the De Jong house."

"Thanks, Moms. I know Jim just has to be doing something besides continually dialing that number." Trixie gathered up the plates. "I'll wash the dishes."

"Don't bother about that. I know Jim is in a hurry to get started."

"It's not far. We can make it in our Bob-White station wagon in no time at all," Brian called. "It's my turn to drive. Hurry, Trix! Have you got your Bob-White jacket?"

Honey met them in the driveway. "Jim was up with the sun. He's out polishing the station wagon for the umpteenth time. Diana and Dan can't go. Jim said Brian is to drive."

"That's right," Trixie said. "Watch Mart crowding into the front seat! That'll make three of them there. Mart, there's all this room in the back. You can even have a seat to yourself."

"And have to listen to you and Honey giggle all the way to the Bronx? No, thanks." Mart edged in next to Jim and shut the car door.

"It's all right with Honey and me," Trixie assured him. "We have plenty to talk about."

"An emergency meeting of the Belden-Wheeler Detective Agency," Mart hooted. "I suppose there's something very mysterious about the fact that Juliana hasn't answered the telephone. We'll probably

see her gagged and blindfolded, being dragged
into a gangster's car—"

"Knock it off, Mart!" Brian ordered. "You can go
too far."

Some time later Mart answered Brian's rebuff.
"You can go too far, too," he remarked, a little
subdued, but still irrepressible. "You'll go so far
you'll pass the De Jong house. I know it's not far
from Castle Hill Avenue, and we passed that."

The De Jong home was a comfortable-looking
brick house set close beside others much like it.
Brian maneuvered the car into the narrow driveway.

"The house has a closed-up look," Trixie said as
they all piled out.

"It sure for certain does," Honey agreed.

They crowded around Trixie as she worked the
old-fashioned bell pull; they heard it jangle far inside the house, then waited.

Nothing stirred.

Trixie pulled again, hard.

No answer.

She turned to the waiting Bob-Whites and
shrugged her shoulders. "Nobody's home."

"That's a brilliant deduction, if I ever heard one,"
Mart said. "Where do we go from here?"

A Surprise for the Bob-Whites • 6

IT WAS a pretty dejected group of Bob-Whites that went down the steps and toward the car.

"Maybe they've all gone somewhere for a vacation," Honey said. "There isn't any mail in the mailbox, though."

"No, I've been taking the De Jongs' mail in for them," a friendly voice said. A pleasant-faced woman came across the yard from the house next door, followed by a little boy. "I'll send it on to them as soon as I have an address. Is there anything I can do for you?"

"It's about Juliana, the girl who lives with them," Honey said. "Do you know anything about her?"

"Of course. Are you friends of hers?"

"I'm her cousin," Jim said. Then, as the woman seemed puzzled, he continued, "I didn't even know she existed till yesterday. I don't think she knew it, either."

"How interesting," the neighbor said. "I'm Mrs. Hendricks. The De Jong family left yesterday for a vacation in the Poconos."

"Did Juliana go, too?" Honey asked quickly.

"No. She had intended to go with them. She changed her mind when she saw an article in a New York newspaper which mentioned her mother's name. It seems there's some land involved, in a little village north of here."

"Sleepyside," Trixie said. "That's where we all live. Where is Juliana now? Nobody answers the doorbell over there." She gestured toward the De Jong home.

"No. Juliana left this morning. She has her own car, a blue Volkswagen. She was going to take care of the business in Westchester County, then join the De Jong family in Pennsylvania. I'm awfully sorry you missed her. Won't you come in for a cold drink before you go back home?"

Trixie shook her head, then looked around at the others.

"We aren't tired, and we haven't far to go," she said. "It's just over the Bronx River Parkway, then the Cross Country to Saw Mill River Road and the

Glen Road exit. It won't take us more than an hour, at the most."

"Girls don't get as thirsty as boys do," Mrs. Hendricks said. "I have two of each myself. Do come in and have a Coke."

"Yes, ma'am!" Mart spoke up before Trixie could shake her head again.

Mrs. Hendricks led the way, laughing. "What is it? What did you say?" she asked as her little boy pulled at her skirt.

"Shall we ask their father to come in, too?" he said in a loud whisper.

Mrs. Hendricks looked up inquiringly.

Trixie shook her head. "No one is with us."

Mrs. Hendricks opened the screen door to a pleasant living room, where the television set was turned on.

"I won't be a minute. Watch the program if you wish. Tommy was watching it. It's the launching of the new spaceship."

"It's just about to blast off," Tommy told them. "See? There's the last of the countdown. Ten, nine, eight, seven, six, five, four, three, two . . . *wowie*! There she goes into orbit—and here's Mom with the Cokes."

They watched till the spaceship became a pin-point of light in the sky and they heard the heroic report from the capsule that everything was "Go!"

For a while they sat and sipped, discussing the

takeoff and—more important to them—Juliana. Mrs. Hendricks seemed very fond of her, and Tommy adored her.

"She gave me some wooden shoes," he said, running upstairs to get them; then he clumped back down wearing them. "Juliana used to live in Holland. I hope she never goes back."

"She's very likely to when she marries," his mother said. "She *is* engaged, you know."

"A letter from their old neighbor in The Hague, Mrs. Schimmel, told us that," Jim said. "I just hope she won't be married very soon. We want a chance to know her." He put down his glass. "Thanks for everything, Mrs. Hendricks, but we'd better be shoving off. We don't know where to look for Juliana in Sleepyside," he explained to their hostess.

"Won't she go right to your home?"

"Not unless she, too, had a letter from Mrs. Schimmel before she left," Jim said. "I doubt that she did."

Honey shook her head positively. "I'm sure she didn't. If she'd had a letter, I'm sure she would have telephoned you, Jim."

"It's all kind of mixed up, you see," Trixie said to Mrs. Hendricks and Tommy, who walked with her to the station wagon.

Inside the car, Brian turned the ignition key. There was no response.

"Now what's wrong?" He tried again.

He and Mart and Jim got out and opened the hood.

"Jeepers!" said Mart.

Brian and Jim just stared. What they saw was nothing but sheer vandalism—a tangle of wires!

"Someone put this car out of business on purpose!" Jim said when he found his voice. "Who could it have been, Mrs. Hendricks? Some smart-aleck kid in the neighborhood?"

"There aren't any smart-aleck kids in this neighborhood," said Mrs. Hendricks with spirit. "There isn't a child older than Tommy for blocks. Anyway, nice people live around here. I should know; I've lived here for ten years. I don't know who would tamper with your car. Can you fix it, do you think?"

"Nobody but a first-rate mechanic could fix that mess," Jim answered, his face red with outrage over the damage.

Honey, disturbed lest Jim offend the neighbor who had been so kind to them, nudged him with her elbow, so he quickly added, "Some wise guy must have gone past while we were inside. He just reached in and grabbed all the wires in sight, just for kicks."

Trixie peered anxiously under the hood, then turned to Mrs. Hendricks. "It's a shame we have to bother you like this."

"What's worse, I'm afraid we'll have to bother you more," Brian said. "May we please use your telephone to call the Automobile Club?"

"Of course," Mrs. Hendricks answered and opened the door for him. "Nothing like this ever happened on our block before."

It was a long time till the mechanic arrived. He shook his head at the damage.

"Can we get going soon?" Jim asked.

"Not for a couple of hours, at least," the man said, puzzled. "Whoever did this must really hate all of you."

"Nobody around here even knows us, so they couldn't hate us," Trixie said.

"Then it must have been some weirdo," the repairman said. "It happens everywhere nowadays. Too often, I'd say."

"Won't you come inside and wait?" Mrs. Hendricks asked the Bob-Whites. "It'll be more fun watching television than just sitting around here."

"Is there a shopping center near here?" Trixie asked. She didn't want to wear out their welcome.

"Three blocks up this street," the neighbor answered. "The stores are interesting, and there's a branch of the Bronx library."

"Let's walk up there then," Trixie said to Honey. "Is it all right, Brian?"

"Sure—but not for more than two hours. When the mechanic gets through here, we get rolling."

"You'd better leave whatever cash you have with me," Jim told Honey. "It might run into money."

It did run into money, and it was late afternoon before the station wagon was in running order again.

"Get in the backseat, please, Mart," Jim suggested as they thanked Mrs. Hendricks, said goodbye to Tommy, and climbed into the station wagon. "I'll do the driving going back, and I like plenty of arm room."

"Yeah, we've had all the bad luck we can take for one day," Mart agreed and climbed obediently into the third seat, stretching out full length.

Trixie, about to climb in behind Jim and Brian, stepped on something hard and turned her ankle. She would have fallen if Honey hadn't caught her.

"Never mind," she said quickly. "Don't get excited, anyone. It didn't hurt me. I just stumbled on this." She held up a brown pipe, handling it gingerly and wrinkling her nose at its smell. Then she threw it into the shrubbery.

"It was probably something Tommy was playing with."

"Or maybe the mechanic left it. Are you sure nothing's wrong?" Brian asked, puzzled by the odd look on Trixie's face. "Does your ankle hurt?"

"No," she answered, and Brian started the car.

When they were on their way, however, Trixie whispered to Honey, "Did you smell that pipe?"

"I can still smell it on your hand," Honey answered under her breath. "Here's a piece of tissue.

Wipe off your hand. Why are we whispering?"

"I've smelled that same tobacco before, that's why."

Honey giggled. "I sometimes agree with Mart. You can make a mystery out of anything, Trixie."

"Maybe I can. But when two unusual things happen together, it can add up to mystery. You don't think all those wires tangled themselves, do you?"

"For pete's sake, quit giggling and talking and let somebody rest, won't you?" Mart complained.

"You're just bothered because you don't know what we're saying."

"Wrong again, Trix," Mart answered. "All I'm interested in just now is food—food with a capital F. I hope Moms has kept something warm for us."

She had—a huge iron kettle of bubbling-hot soup. And there were sandwiches and a big wooden bowl of tangy garden-vegetable salad.

They all gathered around the kitchen sink to wash their hands, crowding and splashing.

"Some of you could use the lavatory in the downstairs bathroom," Trixie's father suggested. "What made you so late?"

They all tried to answer at once, telling about the damage to the car and their long frustrating wait.

"I'll bet you were plenty mad," Bobby said, when they were all at the table, "'specially when you didn't find Juliana there."

Trixie dropped her spoon, almost spilling her

soup. "We haven't told you that yet. How could you possibly know that?"

" 'Cause she's here!" Bobby cried triumphantly.

"Here? Here in this house? Moms, is she?"

"He didn't mean this house," Mrs. Belden said. "I was going to tell you about it as soon as you all settled down a bit. Mrs. Vanderpoel telephoned a while ago to say that Juliana is staying at her house."

"She is?" Trixie cried. "How—"

"She came to Sleepyside today to see about the land that is in her mother's name."

"But how did she wind up at Mrs. Vanderpoel's?" Trixie interrupted, puzzled.

"If you will just let me finish my story—" Mrs. Belden said with a smile.

"I'm sorry, Moms."

"It seems that Juliana went to the newspaper office to inquire and was told that information about her mother had come to them from Mrs. Vanderpoel. So, after she had gone to the office of deeds in the courthouse, she went to see Mrs. Vanderpoel. You know how hospitable she is—and lonesome, too, since Spider Webster and his brother moved away. Well, she invited Juliana to stay at her home while she is here in Sleepyside."

"Jeepers!" Trixie said. "We'll have to get over there and see Juliana. Did Mrs. Vanderpoel say what she was like?"

"Oh, Trixie," Jim said, laughing, "how could she when Juliana was right there, listening? I wonder why she didn't come to our house."

"Probably because she didn't know about you till she talked to Mrs. Vanderpoel."

"Oh, yes, the people at the newspaper showed her the *Sun*," Mrs. Belden said. "Mrs. Schimmel's letter to the courthouse was in it. Your dad read it to you last night. Remember?"

"Then she knows Jim is her cousin and that we're glad to know about her, doesn't she?" Honey asked.

"Yes. Mrs. Vanderpoel said Juliana couldn't wait till she could meet her Cousin Jim."

"Mrs. Belden," Jim said, "do you think we should telephone her or just go over to Mrs. Vanderpoel's house?"

"I think you should take time to finish your supper and then run along. At the rate you're spooning down that soup, you won't even be able to taste it."

"It's sheer starvation that makes me gulp," Jim assured her. "All we had to eat all day was a package of potato chips apiece and a Coke. The De Jongs' neighbor gave us the Coke. We had to put all our money together to pay the mechanic who fixed the car. At that, we barely made it."

"It's too bad the neighbor didn't offer you a bite of something," Mrs. Belden remarked.

"Oh, she did. But we thought we had bothered

her too much already. We told her we brought back some food from the shopping center." Trixie giggled. "We did—the potato chips. It was all the money we had."

At Mrs. Vanderpoel's home, Jim smoothed back his hair, straightened his jacket, and rang the bell.

When the door opened, they all crowded into the big, comfortable living room. "I'm so glad to see you," Mrs. Vanderpoel told them. "I thought you'd never get back to Sleepyside. Juliana's been watching for you."

A tall, slender blond girl came running down, her hands outstretched. "Oh, what a lot of redbirds!" she exclaimed. They were still wearing their Bob-White jackets. "Are you a singing group?"

"No. It's our club, the Bob-Whites of the Glen. I'm Jim—"

"Cousin Jim!" Juliana cried and shook his two hands warmly. "I didn't know I had a Cousin Jim until today. The letter from Mrs. Schimmel didn't reach me before I left the Bronx."

"What a letdown for you," Mart said, laughing. "I'll bet you expected to see a six-footer . . . and a handsome one!"

"Mrs. Vanderpoel told me how nice he is," Juliana said.

Poor Jim's freckled face grew red.

"And what a wonderful group of friends. A club,

you say? You must tell me about it."

"This is Honey, my sister. Her family adopted me," Jim said. "And the Belden family: Trixie, Brian, and Mart. There are two other club members, Diana Lynch and Dan Mangan."

"You'll be seeing enough of us if you're staying awhile," Mart told her as he and Brian and Trixie crowded together on an old Dutch settle.

Juliana's large, bright blue eyes darted from one to another, lingering on Jim's face and Honey's.

"I'll not be here very long," she explained. "Just until I establish my claim to the strip of land that is in my mother's name. Then I shall be going on."

"Yes, we expected that," Jim said. "Mrs. Hendricks said you want to join the De Jong family in the Poconos."

"Mrs. Hendricks?" Juliana looked inquiringly at Honey.

"The De Jongs' next-door neighbor, you know." Juliana nodded.

"I do wish we had reached the Bronx before you left," Honey went on warmly. "Then maybe you would have stayed at our home. Jim would have liked that."

"I hope *you* would have liked it, too, Honey. Mrs. Vanderpoel has been very kind." Juliana smiled at her hostess. "And I shall see you all often, I hope."

"I'm glad as can be to have her here with me," Mrs. Vanderpoel said. "You know how I miss

Spider and Tad Webster. Spider was a policeman in Sleepyside," she explained to Juliana. "Tad is his young brother. I felt so secure when they were here. Then Spider accepted a better position in White Plains. Jim must tell you sometime how Spider helped all of us when the Bob-Whites had their antique show for UNICEF."

"Yes, I'd like to hear about it. In the morning, Cousin Jim, do you think you could take me to the courthouse? There are papers there to sign. I'm sorry I do not have a car. . . ."

"Did something happen to it?" Trixie asked. "Mrs. Hendricks said you drove your own car."

"Oh, yes, this Mrs. Hendricks—she forgot, or did not know, that I put my car in storage and came here by bus. I shall also take the bus when I go to join my friends. Then I can drive back with them, see?"

"Sure," Jim said quickly. "I'll be glad to drive you anywhere you want to go while you're here. You just say the word."

They chatted awhile longer, then Jim renewed his offer to drive his cousin, and they left.

"Wowie!" Mart said as they drove home. " 'Sure, I'll be glad to drive you anywhere, Cousin Juliana,' " he mimicked Jim. "Who wouldn't be? Boy, is she ever neat! A dream from Dreamsville."

"She's beautiful—and so friendly." Honey sighed. "I hope she stays a long, long time."

A Victim of Amnesia • 7

THE NEXT MORNING, as she was dressing, Trixie called to her mother, "Do you know what happened to my white stockings?" She slipped her red and white Candy Striper pinafore over a crisp white blouse.

"They're with the other stockings in the laundry basket," Mrs. Belden answered, stopping in the doorway. "The stockings and socks you were supposed to sort and put away."

"Oh, Moms, I did forget. I've had a million things to think about lately. Moms—"

"Yes?"

"Jim's cousin is one of the most beautiful girls I

ever saw, and so nice. No wonder Mrs. Schimmel was fond of her, especially when she practically raised her. She wears her hair straight back from her forehead, like this." Trixie struggled to straighten her unruly short curls. "I *wish* I had been born with straight hair. The only place curly hair looks good is on poodles."

"I like your hair the way it is. Here are your stockings. I'll ask Bobby to sort the rest of them. You'd better run now. Honey will be waiting for you."

"We're taking our bikes. I'll probably stop at Honey's house on the way back, that is if the other Bob-Whites are there. 'Bye, Moms!"

It was a lovely, crisp, sunny morning in late summer. Sumac was just beginning to redden around the edges—the first reminder, Trixie thought, that summer was waning and soon junior-senior high would begin its fall semester.

Her thoughts raced on as she pedaled her way along Glen Road. At the turn near Manor House, she met Jim just leaving in the station wagon. He was going to pick up Juliana, she knew. They would go on to the courthouse to look after his cousin's business.

There wasn't another person in the world like Jim. He never once even thought of the large sum of money that would have been his if Juliana hadn't shown up. Trixie was sure of this. Money didn't

seem to mean a thing to him. He'd even forgotten
the half million dollars his great-uncle had left him.
Well, maybe he hadn't forgotten it, but certainly
he never thought of using it for anything except
the school for runaway boys he planned for the
future, when he had finished college.

Trixie thought of the frightened runaway Jim
himself had been when she and Honey first found
him hiding in the old abandoned mansion that had
belonged to his great-uncle. He was hiding from
that Jones man, his stepfather. It was terrible that
anyone could have been as mean as his stepfather
had been to Jim— *especially* Jim. He was just the
greatest.

So engrossed was Trixie in the memory of that
unhappy time that she bumped her bike into the
veranda step at Manor House and almost fell.

Honey, waiting in her Candy Striper uniform,
ran to help her. "Did you hurt yourself?" she asked.
"Weren't you watching where you were going?"

"Huh-uh." Trixie shook her head. "I was thinking
of so many things. My mind was miles away. Don't
you wish that the Bob-Whites could just go on and
on as we are now, just the same age we are now?"

"Heavens! What makes you so serious? It isn't
like you, Trixie, especially on such a pretty day.
Did you meet Jim as he drove away?"

"Yes. I guess I was thinking about him and about
Juliana and about . . . oh, just everything. I'm to

take the book cart around today, Honey. What are you going to do?"

"Scrub up, I guess. I always get to do some scrubbing. I don't mind."

Chatting, planning, and sometimes silent, the two girls rode down Glen Road into the little town of Sleepyside and around a corner to where the hospital stood.

The morning was to be far from routine.

Trixie didn't take the book cart around, and Honey didn't do any scrubbing up. Instead something happened that was to affect their lives profoundly for a long time to come.

All the way home they said little; there was so much to tell, but it could wait until the Bob-Whites all got together.

"Stay for lunch," Honey begged Trixie as, flushed and excited, they parked their bikes in the driveway at Manor House. "Jim's back; the Bob-White station wagon is here. Maybe Mart and Brian are here, too. Not one of them will believe what we have to tell them!"

As it turned out, their news would have to wait even longer.

As they rushed inside, breathless, the girls found Miss Trask and the boys, with Juliana, at the luncheon table. Juliana's voice sounded high and complaining.

"Those men in the courthouse couldn't give me the slightest idea of when my claim could be settled. They didn't seem to care *when* I get away from Sleepyside. It may be weeks!"

"It won't be," Jim told her soothingly, then went on to explain to Honey and Trixie. "They have to write to The Hague for some affadavits."

"It'll take forever," Juliana moaned.

"It only took one week for Trixie to have an answer to *her* letter. Cheer up, Juliana," Jim said. "We can do lots of things to have fun. Before you know it, the papers will be here."

Juliana shrugged her shoulders. "I *have* to get finished and go on to meet my friends."

"I only went to the Poconos once," Mart said. "I'll tell you, I'd a lot rather be right here in Sleepyside."

"Me, too," Brian agreed.

Juliana, seemingly aware that she had sounded ungracious, said quickly, "I didn't mean to be unappreciative. I like to be here, but. . . ." She changed the subject. "What did you and Trixie do at the hospital today, Honey?"

"We found everyone in an uproar," Trixie began dramatically, taking quick advantage of the chance to tell their exciting story. "Yesterday the police found a girl unconscious on Glen Road!"

She looked around at the shocked faces and went on. "She's about your age, Juliana, I think, though she does look younger. Oh, I don't mean that you look old. . . . I'm so mixed up I don't know what I mean. I saw the girl. So did Honey. Someone must have hit her with a car and just kept going."

"How shameful!" Miss Trask said. "Was she badly injured?"

Honey shook her head. "I don't think so; do you, Trixie?"

"No. Otherwise they wouldn't have let us see her at all. She was in a coma for several hours. It was a concussion, the doctor said. She'll be all right physically in a few days. That isn't the worst problem. The worst is that she doesn't even know her own name or where she came from— Oh, Juliana, I'm sorry. I've frightened you. It *is* a terrible thing to think about."

"Don't worry about me," Juliana said faintly. She did look pale. "It's warm in here. May I open the door?"

"The house is air-conditioned," Miss Trask told Juliana. "Maybe you'd better turn down the thermostat, Jim."

"I'll be all right," Juliana insisted. "Go on, please, Trixie. This girl—doesn't anyone know who she is?"

Trixie shook her head. "The police have reported it to the Bureau of Missing Persons."

"And they found that she isn't listed there," Honey added. "The accident happened right near Ten Acres, Jim, where your great-uncle's house used to be. It's a lonely place since Ten Acres burned."

"I've thought for a long time that there should be extra lights there," Miss Trask said. "There's no sidewalk on Glen Road, either—not even a footpath."

"The police said she might have been injured someplace else and dropped off near Ten Acres," Honey said. "It'll be in the paper this evening, I suppose. That's the trouble when a newspaper doesn't come out every day. News is usually a day old before it's published in the *Sun*."

"The girl seemed so nervous and looked so white," Trixie said. "Imagine not remembering your own name."

"Did she remember other things?" Juliana asked.

"Like what?" Trixie asked.

"Who her friends were. How the accident happened. Anything."

"She doesn't remember a thing about any accident, and she hasn't the slightest idea what she was doing in Sleepyside. She doesn't remember ever having heard of our town before. She seems well educated, and the nurse said the clothes she wore were pretty."

"Leave it to Detective Belden to find out all the details," Mart teased.

"Detective?" Juliana asked. "Detective Belden? Is your father a detective?"

"Nope," Mart answered, "Trixie is—and Honey. They're the Belden-Wheeler Detective Agency; at least they expect to be, when they're older."

"I see," Juliana said with a sigh, "just kid stuff." She looked narrowly at Trixie. "You *do* seem to have a way of ferreting things out."

"It's not 'kid stuff,'" Mart corrected her. He was swift to spring to his sister's defense, just as he was quick to tease and needle her. "Several pretty important cases would have gone unsolved if Trixie and Honey hadn't helped the police and federal agents. They've even won cash awards for our Bob-White club fund."

Juliana smiled indulgently. "I'm sure that must be so. Miss Trask, have you known of this agency?"

"I surely have," Miss Trask said firmly. "I've not only known about it, but I've also been right there with the girls several times when they have unraveled a really difficult mystery—the jewel robbery in New York, for instance. I've seen them in operation. *I* don't make fun of them."

Hurrah for Miss Trask, Trixie thought. She *never* let the Bob-Whites down. Juliana didn't have to be so sarcastic, either. Oh, well, maybe she hadn't meant it that way. Other people hadn't been too impressed, either, with a detective agency made up of two young girls—until they came bang up against some of their achievements. Sergeant Molinson, head of the Sleepyside police, was still sarcastic, and he had reason to know better.

"I didn't intend to make fun of them," Juliana said, so humbly that everyone forgave her. "And I think it is very unselfish of the girls to do volunteer work at the hospital. I'll have time on my hands until that letter comes through from Holland. Maybe there's something I can do. Do you think that I might go to the hospital to see this girl? What do they call her, since she can't remember her name?"

"Janie," Trixie said. "Dr. Gregory and the nurses gave her the name. It seems to fit her, even though she shakes her head and says she's sure it isn't her name. But, Juliana, I really can't think of anything you could do at the hospital in the short time that you'll be here."

"Couldn't I take her some flowers?" Juliana suggested. "Maybe read to your Janie?"

"I don't see why not," Honey answered. "Do you, Trixie?"

"She can read, herself," Trixie said. "There's nothing the matter with her mind, they told us. You might visit Janie, though," she added quickly, "if it's all right. We'll have to ask at the hospital."

The girls did inquire and were assured by the head nurse that Janie seemed lonely and restless, and that it might do her good to have visitors.

So the next day, her arms full of roses from the

Manor House garden, Juliana went to Sleepyside Hospital with the girls. Jim drove them.

They found Janie sitting by herself on a chintz-covered sofa in the pleasant solarium on the second floor.

Sure that Mrs. Wheeler would have wanted her to do so, and urged on by Honey, Miss Trask had thoughtfully provided needed clothing for Janie. The girl made a pretty picture in a leaf-green linen dress which accentuated her lovely blond hair, close-cropped by the doctor to make way for the white bandage wound round her head.

She looked up expectantly as the three girls greeted her.

"This is Juliana Maasden," Honey told her. "She is my brother's cousin. She lives in the Bronx. She used to live in Holland, in The Hague."

A frown crossed Janie's face and quickly disappeared. "How good to know one's own name and where one lives," she said to Juliana. "*I don't*, you know."

"The doctor promises that you *will* remember, Janie, so don't worry about it. Relax." Trixie put the roses in water and held the vase so Janie could see it. "Aren't they beautiful? They're from the Wheelers' garden."

"Juliana was the one who thought about bringing them to you," Honey said generously.

"That was kind of you," Janie said gratefully.

"One thing I do remember . . . I love flowers."

"Have you had any report at all from the inquiries that are being made about you?" Juliana asked, seating herself on a wicker seat near Janie. "It seems so strange. . . ."

"Yes, doesn't it?" Janie's eyes saddened. "There hasn't been a word from the Missing Persons Bureau. I guess nobody has lost a girl like me," she added wistfully.

"Losers weepers, finders keepers," Trixie chanted and put her arm around Janie's shoulder. "We've *found* something, haven't we, Honey? A friend."

Janie smiled. Color rushed to her cheeks. She put her hand up to clasp Trixie's.

"I hope I may be your friend, too," Juliana said. "Is it true, Janie, that you don't remember one thing that happened at the time of your accident?"

Janie shook her head. Sadness had returned to her lovely blue eyes.

Honey, sitting at Juliana's side on the wicker seat, whispered low, "The doctor thinks it is better not to talk too much about the accident."

Juliana must not have heard Honey's whisper, for she went on probing. "Were you walking along the road and struck by an automobile?"

"I don't . . . just don't . . . remember," Janie answered.

"Do you try to remember? It was an automobile that struck you, wasn't it? It almost had to be."

Janie put her hand to her head and winced. "It hurts to try to remember, but I have to do it."

"You don't have to try at all, Janie," Trixie said calmly. "The doctor says it will all come rushing back to you at once, and trying hard is the worst thing you can do. So you see, Juliana, we'd better not ask questions. I think we'd better be going now."

Juliana didn't have anything more to say until they were out of the hospital and Jim was driving them back home.

Then she said reprovingly, "You should have told me the doctor said not to question her, Trixie. Then you wouldn't have had to scold me in front of Janie."

Trixie was immediately repentant. "I didn't mean it to sound that way. I was feeling so sorry for Janie that I just didn't stop to think what it might sound like to anyone else."

"I *did* whisper to you not to question Janie," Honey reminded Juliana. "I guess you didn't hear me."

"What's all the discussion about?" Jim asked. "Has the girl remembered who she is?"

"No, she hasn't," Juliana said, "and I guess I committed a major crime. . . ."

Embarrassed, Trixie reassured her. "It was only natural for you to try to help her remember, Juliana. It was our fault for not telling you what the doctor said. We should have made sure you heard Honey."

"Forget the whole thing!" Juliana said. "It's a case of misunderstanding. I'm so full of my own problems that I'm nervous and edgy. I'm sorry. Let's forget it."

Trixie forgot it—or tried to. She knew how Jim hated any kind of controversy, so she changed the subject.

"Just drop me off at Crabapple Farm, please, Jim," she said. "Di is bringing her twin brothers to our house to play with Bobby. That surely means I'll have to help Moms keep an eye on them."

"Will you mind if I stop off with you, too?" Juliana asked. "I like boys . . . little ones especially. I have to do something to pass the time. I can at least read to the boys."

Janie Might Be Dangerous! • 8

THAT EVENING Trixie looked up as she was putting the cloth on the table. "Moms?"

"Yes, what is it, Trixie?"

"I don't know what's the matter with me sometimes."

"What's troubling you now?"

"I get crazy ideas about people. Maybe being a detective makes me sort of suspicious of everyone. This morning, for instance, when Juliana went to the hospital with Honey and me. . . ."

"Yes?"

"Oh, it's hard to explain, but she seemed to be trying to make Janie more nervous and confused instead of better. She kept asking her so many questions."

"Did Janie object?"

"She didn't object, exactly, but she was sort of bewildered. It seemed to me that Juliana knew this but kept on asking—almost as though she wanted to be ... mean."

"That's a harsh word."

"I know it is. I told you it's hard to explain the feeling I had. It makes me ashamed, because look how wonderful she was this afternoon with Larry and Jerry Lynch and Bobby! Who else would have thought to ask Dan to ride Spartan over here so the boys could see him dance? They loved it. Dan thinks she's one hundred percent perfect."

Mrs. Belden laughed. "She doesn't sound like a 'mean' person. I wonder—is it Juliana who rubs you the wrong way, or would you feel the same about anyone who upset your Bob-White activities?"

"Oh, Moms, I hope I'm not that selfish. I don't feel that way about everybody—not about Janie. Everybody loves Janie."

"Does Honey have this impression of Juliana? Does Jim?"

"Of course Jim doesn't. She's his cousin. I haven't said anything to them about it. I guess it's just me. Forget it!"

Mrs. Belden opened the door to let Reddy out in response to Bobby's whistle. "You forget it,

Trixie. Whatever the feeling is, it will pass away. I've been thinking about something else. Since Janie seems to be greatly recovered physically, do you think it would help this amnesia if she'd get away from the hospital, away from the atmosphere of sickness?"

"Oh, Moms, it would! It would! It would help her more than anything. Do you think we could possibly—"

"Invite her to stay with us for a while at Crabapple Farm? This is exactly what I had in mind. I thought I'd ask the doctor about it tomorrow morning. I've already talked it over with your dad. He thinks, as I do, that wholesome food, lots of fresh air, walks in the woods, normal people around her— all of it could help Janie. I'll see if Dr. Gregory agrees."

In the morning Mrs. Belden took Bobby to White Plains to do some shopping.

"I'll stop at the hospital first thing and talk to Dr. Gregory," she told Trixie. "They may let me bring Janie home with me later on."

"Perfect! Do you think they will?"

"It's possible. Oh, dear, I meant to dust the downstairs bedroom. The sheets have been changed, but the room does need more cleaning. Maybe I'd better wait till tomorrow to see about Janie coming here."

"No! No! I can clean the room. The boys will help me."

"Oh, we will, will we?" Mart asked. "Who says so?"

"I do," his mother answered. "It won't take long. You want Janie to come here, don't you?"

"Of course, Moms. Oh, all right! All right!"

The big old-fashioned farmhouse was ideally arranged to provide a maximum of privacy for a guest. An extra room and bath had been built downstairs for Trixie's father and mother just after they had married. A few years later, both grandparents died. Now the room housed Mr. Belden's occasional business guests and, from time to time, the children's guests.

A big picture window looked out on Mrs. Belden's rose garden. She had taken prizes at the county fair, especially for the corner garden of old-fashioned yellow banksias, which trailed along the white picket fence, and bushes of sweet-scented moss roses. These were an inheritance from Mr. Belden's mother and had grown in the same spot for over half a century.

The room itself had been recently refurnished and was gay with yellow-flowered chintz and pale green walls. The furniture was pine, with twin spool beds, bookcases and a matching desk—an inviting room, and one in which Trixie hoped Janie would be happy and grow strong and well.

When Mrs. Belden and Bobby left, the dust began to fly. The boys carried the rug from the guest room and out onto the grass to beat it.

"Whack!" Brian wielded the rattan beater. "There's one for the guy in the Bronx who put our Bob-White bus on the blink!"

"Whack!" said Mart. "Another for the goon Trixie saw down at the marsh."

"They're both the same person," Trixie said, giving the dust mop a vigorous shake in Mart's direction. "It was his pipe I found, too, after he jangled those wires on our car."

Brian laughed. "You and your one-track mind."

"Yeah, Trixie the Schoolgirl Shamus," Mart teased. "Where did all this dust come from, anyway? Don't you and Moms ever clean that room?"

"We can't take the rug out and beat it every time you and Bobby and Brian tramp dust in there. If you'd ever come in the back door, the way Moms keeps telling you to, and use the mat—"

"Forget it!" Mart told her as he and Brian folded the rug. "Is the floor all waxed and ready to accept this superclean job?"

"It is. Will you help me take down the curtains from my room and trade them for those in the guest room?"

"For pete's sake, what's the matter with the ones that are hanging there now?" Mart asked.

"Mine are prettier. I want the room to be perfect

for Janie. What do you have to do that's so terribly important that you can't help me?"

"I have to have some time to practice catching balls."

"All right, then, Brian will help me."

"And who will pitch the balls? Reddy?"

"Try him. He's pretty smart. There's one thing I know, and that is that I promised Moms to have this room ready, and she said you were to help me."

"We are helping you, aren't we?"

"Yes, but I can sense mutiny in the air. Mart, this mat has to be centered." She gave the pretty hooked rug a tug. "There! Now, Brian, you lift one end of the bed while Mart and I try to roll the rug under it. Then you'll have to help me put the dresser and desk back in place."

"Goll!" Brian protested. "You're more of a slave driver than Moms. I'd sure hate to be the guy that you marry."

"Why?" Mart asked unexpectedly. "Trixie is already a good cook, and, boy, does this room look neat!"

He stood off, dusting his hands. "There should be some flowers on that desk, shouldn't there?"

"I'll get 'em," Brian said and came back soon with a conglomerate bunch of colors—zinnias, marigolds, late, fragrant pinks. He thrust them into a squat Bennington jar, where they looked amazingly appropriate and colorful. "I just hope Janie appreciates all this toil," he said. "Oh, my aching back!"

"She will. You'll see," Trixie said. "It's going to be wonderful having her here and helping her get well."

"Trixie, the Florence Nightingale of modern New England!"

"Oh, yes?" Trixie smiled. "You pretend to be so hardhearted, Mart. You're just an old softie. You're glad she's coming here, and you know it."

"Who wouldn't want to help a girl who's in a jam like she is? She doesn't even know where her family is. She doesn't even know if she has one or not. It beats me why someone isn't looking for her. Oh, yikes!" he groaned. "Look who's coming up the drive now—Juliana! We'll have to put her to work."

"I don't think so," Brian said. "She doesn't seem to be the working kind. Look how dressed up she is."

They all went out to greet her.

"I didn't hear Reddy bark, and I didn't see your mother's car. I thought perhaps nobody was at home."

"I'll say we are," Mart said, "beating rugs, moving furniture. You're just in time to help."

"Don't pay any attention to Mart," Trixie said. "We're through with the hard part of the work. Janie is coming here to stay with us for a while. We're hoping it will help her get well. Moms and

Bobby have gone to the hospital to get her."

"Janie ... is ... coming ... here?" Juliana gasped.

"Yes. She can take walks in the woods, and Moms will feed her good food, and—" Trixie leaned over to pick up one of Bobby's toys from the walk. "What makes you so surprised?"

"I'm not surprised. I'm shocked! Did the doctor say she could leave the hospital?"

"Moms is going to ask him. She won't bring her home unless Dr. Gregory says it's all right. Why?"

"Why? She might be dangerous, that's why! She could suddenly go crazy and hurt someone."

The idea seemed so preposterous to the Beldens that the boys burst out laughing.

"There's nothing the matter with Janie's mind," Trixie said with spirit. "People with amnesia are not dangerous. And Janie's so little. No wonder Mart and Brian are laughing. Janie probably doesn't weigh much more than a hundred pounds. How could she hurt any—"

"So even if she were a black belt karate expert, she could hardly take on Bobby," Mart said, still laughing. "She's liable to be here soon, Juliana, so if you're afraid. . . ."

"I can go back to Mrs. Vanderpoel's. Is that what you mean, Mart? Well, I *can* go back and I'm going. You may regret what you're doing." She turned to go.

"Don't be cross with us," Trixie called after her.

"We shouldn't have laughed at you, but, honestly, Janie isn't. . . ."

"She can't hear you. She's so mad she's practically running," Mart told Trixie. "Gol, is she some kind of a kook herself?"

"I don't know. Gleeps, Mart," Trixie said, "she was so serious."

"Lost memory dangerous?" Brian snorted. "Anyone with half a head knows better than that."

"You know it because you're going to be a doctor. Let's give Juliana a break. She *is* Jim's cousin, and we *did* make fun of her. Moms won't like that if she hears about it." Trixie glanced at the clock as Reddy barked excitedly—as usual when he recognized the sound of the Belden car approaching.

Jeepers, she thought frantically, *I only had time to butter the bread and put it in the oven to toast.* She looked in the mirror over the stove. "Mrs. Witch in person," she groaned. "Oh, well, the room's ready."

Quickly she whisked blue homespun mats from the kitchen drawer, put them on the old maple drop leaf table, then added silver and yellow paper napkins. Moms would have something ready to eat in no time, she thought as she toweled her face till it shone and brushed back her sandy curls.

"Welcome to Crabapple Farm!" she called to the slender girl who came in with Mrs. Belden, followed by Mart and Brian carrying boxes.

Inside the kitchen Janie stood quiet, sniffed the fragrant toast, saw the sprigged curtains stirring in the breeze from the garden, and let her eyes wander to the hospitable table with its ladder-back chairs pushed in and waiting.

She saw Trixie, red-faced and radiant, felt the brush of Reddy's wagging tail, saw the boys disappearing down the hall with her possessions, and tightened her hold on Bobby's hand. "It's all so wonderful," she sighed. "Why are you so good to me?"

"We want you to get well," Mrs. Belden said briskly. "Trixie, take Janie back to her room. I'll have some salad and soup on the table in a minute. Bobby, take Reddy outside, please. No dogs in the house when we are eating, remember?"

"Reddy's not a dog," Bobby pouted. "He's part of the family."

"Then part of the family will eat lunch outside." Mrs. Belden handed Bobby Reddy's dish. "I added a little of that cat food he's so crazy about. After all, he's entitled to something special, too, because Janie's here." She ran her hand lovingly over Bobby's cowlicked hair.

"When do we eat, Moms?" Mart asked, pretending to puff from the weight of Janie's box he had carried. "Where'd she get all those things, anyway? All she had was what she had on when she was found—"

"Shhhh!" Mrs. Belden warned. "Honey's mother told Miss Trask to buy the things Janie needed," she added in a quiet voice. "Oh, I do hope she'll be happy here."

"And gets well soon," Bobby added, slamming the screen door.

"Amen to hoping Janie will get well, but why can't Bobby ever learn to close a door without a bang?" Mart asked.

"He'll learn it the same way you and Brian did," Mrs. Belden said and told both the boys to wash their hands at the kitchen sink.

"See, smarty?" Bobby jeered.

"Oh, yeah?" Mart answered and pulled the chair out from under his brother, dropping him to the floor, howling.

"Mart, pick Bobby up immediately," his mother said, "and all of you, for goodness' sake, stop yelling at one another."

"You see?" Trixie said to Janie, who had come in from her room. "It isn't all sweetness and light at the Belden homestead."

"Who's perfect all the time?" Janie answered, smiling, and won the boys' hearts. "That's the loveliest room, Mrs. Belden—and the view!"

"Trixie and the boys put it in order," Mrs. Belden answered. "Just sit anywhere, Janie . . . maybe over there next to Bobby. Then there won't be any squabbling about 'who's sitting in my chair?' "

"That's what the bears said," Bobby told Janie
and handed her the napkin-covered basket of crisp
toast.

"I faintly remember reading something like that
about fifteen years ago," Janie said, smiling.

"The salad's from our garden," Bobby said. "Take
a lot of it, Janie. We have it every day. Hey, Trixie,
there comes Honey on her bike. Just listen to Reddy
barking."

What Happens to Missing People? • 9

WHY DIDN'T YOU let me know Janie was coming?"
Honey asked. "I'd have helped you get ready."

The luncheon dishes were done, and, at Mrs.
Belden's suggestion, Janie had gone to her room
to rest.

Honey and Trixie were in Trixie's room upstairs.
How she loved this room of her own and Moms's
inflexible rule: No one enters a room with a closed
door without knocking. Here was privacy, a rare
thing in a household of young people, and it was
greatly treasured.

"I'd have let you know she was coming," Trixie
said, "but I wasn't sure—not really sure—till she

came home with Moms. Anyway, Mart and Brian helped me get the room ready. Oh, Honey, do you think she will be happy here?"

"It's a perfect place for her." Honey's eyes shone. "I wouldn't mind losing my memory, if I could stay for a while at Crabapple Farm."

"Anytime . . . any old time you want to come," Trixie said, putting her arm around her friend. "I wish I could *really* do something to help Janie . . . soon; she looks so white and thin. Oh, I know what you're going to say: Moms's food will soon change that. That's true, but there's much more to it."

"She keeps worrying about not knowing who she is," Honey said sadly. "I know what you mean. I don't know what anyone can do about that—I mean anything we haven't already done."

"She's so helpless. Honey, we can't just play around this afternoon. We have to start doing what we can for her. I know! I'll ask Moms if I can go to the library. We can ride our bikes."

"What could we do there?"

"Look over every inch of the *New York Times* for at least ten days back—see if we can find any item about a missing person."

"Don't you think the Missing Persons Bureau would know that before a news story could get into the *New York Times?*"

"Maybe so. Maybe they would. But with so many people disappearing all the time, they could overlook something. It's worth trying. Miss Trask won't care if you go, will she?"

"Not if your mother thinks it's all right. Shall we ask her?"

"We'll just ask if we can go to the library. She might think we were silly to look through the newspaper. I'm sure the boys would think so if she told them."

Mrs. Belden had no objection. "You may go—if you think you can get your bike out of the barn and get away without Bobby seeing you. Lately he thinks he has to go along with anyone who leaves this house. He's back in the pasture with Reddy now, so hurry!"

The two girls pedaled rapidly to the top of the hill, then coasted their bikes down into the village. They parked them in the rack outside the library and went into the reading room.

"May we please see late copies of the *New York Times*?" Trixie asked.

"Help yourself, girls," the librarian answered. "They're hanging on that rack over there—this week's editions. If you want to go back farther than that, reach into the shelf right back of the rack."

They carried copy after copy to the long table and ran their fingers down each column looking for news of accidents or missing people, following through on any item that seemed to have any promise. Aside from the small notice about the dredging of the marshland, which Honey found, there was no other mention of Sleepyside.

"I didn't think we'd find anything," Honey said sadly. "After all, the police all over the state of New York have been notified. . . . What *are* you staring at, Trixie?"

"This!" Trixie said aloud, and the librarian held up a warning finger. "Look, Honey." She spread out a copy of a small newspaper from Lakeside, Illinois, a Chicago suburb.

"That man who was sitting across the table from us left it," she told Honey excitedly. "And I saw this headline. It may mean something."

Honey read the headline: WHAT HAPPENS TO MISSING PEOPLE?

In response to a roving reporter's questions, several people had given their answers. Trixie's eyes fairly popped from her head as she huddled close to Honey, reading.

The picture of one woman, and her answer, stood out as though it were in boldface type.

The woman's name, Beth Meredith, was given, and her address. In an excited whisper, Trixie read Beth Meredith's answer to the query:

> "Ten days ago my younger sister, Barbara Crane, went to the southern part of New York State to take her first teaching job. She promised to write or call the minute she found a place to stay. I haven't heard a word from her. Today I

called the president of the school board, and he said she had not reported to him. What *do* people do to trace missing people?"

"It's Janie!" both girls shouted.

"Shhhh!" the librarian warned.

"Let's go outside where we *can* talk," Trixie whispered. "Wait. I'll copy the name and address."

Outside, Trixie found herself trembling. "It's Janie . . . I know it is! What shall we do?"

"Find out how much money we have between us," Honey said. "If there's enough, we can telephone to Lakeside."

"See how smart you are? And you're always saying I'm the brains of our agency. Oh, Honey, my fingers are all thumbs."

Trixie spilled the contents of her coin purse on the steps between them. "You count it. We'll have to call person-to-person. That'll mean more money."

"We have a lot." Honey laughed. "There's almost two dollars in my purse and . . . heavens! . . . nearly four dollars in yours!"

"Part of that belongs to Moms. I was supposed to pay the laundryman this morning, and he didn't come. Moms would never mind, I know, if we had to use it. Let's find a telephone booth—one outside the library. She'd just start shushing us again."

"There's one across the street at the filling station." Honey put all the money together in Trixie's purse. "We can try it."

They hurried across, leaving their bikes in the library rack.

"You do the calling, Trixie," Honey insisted. "You'll know what to say."

"I'm shaking so I can't even dial the operator. Here, hold this purse and take out the coins so I can drop them in when I get the connection . . . if I do. Oh, jeepers, Honey, just think—"

The operator asked for the deposit, heard the correct amount being inserted, then said, "I have your party on the line. Go ahead, please."

"Oh, Mrs. Meredith! I'm Trixie Belden, and I live in Sleepyside, New York. You don't know me, but that's who I am, and my friend Honey Wheeler is standing right here beside me. Oh, dear . . . that doesn't mean anything to you, but *I hope I know your sister!*"

"Oh, heavens!" the voice answered. "You think you know Barbara? Wait a minute till I get a chair. I feel faint. Is Barbara all right?"

"Oh, I do hope so. You see, it was this way. . . ." Trixie told her of Janie's accident and described her. "She did have long, blond hair before they had to cut it very short because of the bump on her head."

"Oh, dear! Please, go on."

"She wasn't seriously hurt. I think it was an accident. Nobody seems to know. Her head is all right now . . . well, no, it isn't. . . ."

"What do you mean? You sound incoherent."

"I'm sorry. What I'm trying to say is that your sister—I hope she *is* your sister; we call her Janie—she's completely well, except that she has lost her memory. The doctors don't think it's serious. She *is* well, physically, Mrs. Meredith."

"You mean she's not well *mentally?* Oh, dear!"

"No, Mrs. Meredith . . . please . . . she is all right. The doctor doesn't think her loss of memory is serious. She was released from the hospital and is staying at our home, Crabapple Farm, just outside of Sleepyside, New York. I'll give you our telephone number, but please give me a chance to get back there before you call her. My friend and I just found a copy of your Lakeside newspaper in our library. We saw the interview you gave the reporter, and that's why we called. Please call this number—" Trixie recited her home phone number— "in about half an hour, will you?"

"Your three minutes are up . . . please deposit—"

The receiver at the other end of the line clicked.

"She hung up," Trixie said, dejected. "I guess I did sound kind of wild. She must have thought I was crazy. We'd better get home as quickly as we can, Honey, before she telephones our house. Moms won't have the slightest idea what it's all about."

The girls fairly ran up the hill from the library, pushing their bikes ahead. Then, on level ground, they pedaled as fast as their feet would fly down

Glen Road and into the driveway at Crabapple
Farm. They dropped their bikes and ran into the
house.

"Did she call?" Trixie cried. "Did she talk to
Janie?"

"Trixie! Calm down!" her mother ordered. "Did
who call whom?"

"Did Mrs. Meredith call her sister Janie . . . I
mean Barbara?"

"Janie's not Barbara," Bobby said.

"She is! She is! I know she is. I'm practically certain she is," Trixie insisted, stumbling over the
words in her excitement.

"Now, Trixie, take it easy. Honey, you're just as
excited. Whatever could have happened? Take
your time and tell me what this is all about—slowly,
please," her mother said.

"I . . . have to . . . tell . . . Janie, too," Trixie
gasped. "Where is she?"

"I'm here, Trixie. What happened?"

"I've just talked on the telephone to your sister,
Janie—I mean, you are really Barbara."

She looked expectantly at Janie, who only
seemed confused.

"My sister? I don't understand."

"Your sister Beth—Beth Meredith— Oh, Janie,
doesn't the name Barbara, Barbara Crane, mean a
thing to you? Or your sister's name, Beth, Beth
Meredith?"

Janie shook her head slowly and dropped into a chair. "Should it mean something, Trixie? Am I Barbara?"

"I *think* you are. Honey and I both think you are, don't we, Honey?"

"We do, Janie. We think you are Barbara and your home is in Lakeside, Illinois. Oh, Janie . . . think! Lakeside . . . Lakeside. . . ."

Janie shook her head sadly, tears welling up in her eyes. "I don't understand anything you're trying to tell me."

"Of course she doesn't, girls. Look, you even have Bobby whimpering. Say what you have to say, slowly and coherently." Mrs. Belden took Janie's hand. "Begin at the beginning, Trixie."

So Trixie explained in detail to Janie just what had happened at the library and how sure she and Honey were that they had uncovered the secret of Janie's real name.

She had hardly finished when the telephone bell shrilled.

"That will be Mrs. Meredith, Moms—Janie's sister—calling her. You'd better answer it," Trixie begged. "She thinks I'm off my rocker."

"She's sitting right here," Mrs. Belden said after she had talked to Mrs. Meredith and the woman had quieted down. "I'll let her talk to you now."

Janie talked. But she didn't remember—not one single thing.

"I never heard that voice before in all my life," she said tearfully as she replaced the receiver. "She seemed certain I am her sister. I did like her voice. But I . . . don't . . . remember. She said she would talk to her husband when he came home and they would call me again later. I don't remember him, either."

"Don't worry about it, Janie," Honey said, and she put her arms around her. "My dad will be home tonight," Honey went on. "He has his own plane. I know he'll fly you to Lakeside, and when you actually see your sister Beth, you'll remember. Don't you think that's a good idea, Mrs. Belden?"

"It will be perfect, if your father will have time to do it. Bobby, will you *please* take Reddy outside and stop pulling at my arm? I can't talk to more than one person at a time."

"I only wanted to ask if I can . . . may . . . go on the plane with Janie and Honey."

"I might have known. It's a wonder you don't want Reddy to go, too. I'm pretty sure there won't be room for you, Bobby. We aren't even sure Mr. Wheeler will be able to make the trip."

"I am," Honey said. "I'm sure Dad will *take* the time to fly Janie to Lakeside." Honey's voice was confident. "I think Bobby may go, too—but not Reddy," she added quickly.

"He's outside, and he didn't hear you say I c'd go, so that's all right," Bobby shouted. "I'm going home with you, Janie. I'm going home with you!"

"That's . . . good . . . Bobby. I hope it will be . . . home!" Janie jumped up, tears streaming down her face, and ran to her room.

"What's the matter with Janie, Moms?" Bobby asked.

"She's upset. She's nervous. Bobby, there are times when you are decidedly *de trop!*"

"What does that mean?" Bobby asked Trixie as she and Honey and her mother followed Janie.

"I don't know, but I think it means get lost," Trixie said, giving Bobby an affectionate pat and a little shove toward the door.

"Of course, the whole thing has been a deep shock to Janie," Mrs. Belden told Trixie later. They were back in the kitchen. "She's gone for a walk. She loves the woods. Now don't ask me again if I warned her not to go beyond the signs near the edge of the cliff. I always warn her about that. Anyway, she probably won't go that far.

"I'm proud of you, Trixie, proud of you and Honey. What a coincidence that you saw that column in the newspaper. I think I'd better talk to Dr. Gregory and tell him what has happened. He may want me to give Janie some instructions about her medication. Perhaps I'd better call him right now. Then when she comes back from her walk, she can rest before dinner."

It was a different Janie who came to the dinner table. She seemed more at peace somehow.

"I *hope* I'm found," she said as Brian held her chair. "My sister's husband"—her voice weakened and then gathered strength—"called and said they would arrive here in Sleepyside sometime tomorrow evening."

"But Honey's father is going to take you home in the morning, and I'm going, too," Bobby said quickly. "Or aren't I, Moms?" he added plaintively.

"I told him that," Janie said, "but I had to tell him that I wouldn't be certain till Honey's father gets home."

"He'll go, all right," Trixie said. "He *always* does what Honey and Jim ask him to do . . . if he can."

"That's still 'iffy,' " Mart said. "And, Trixie, stop thinking for Mr. Wheeler!"

"Hmph!" said Trixie. "At least I—"

"Trixie! Mart!" Mr. Belden said sternly.

"This is a time when we should all be happy with Janie," Mrs. Belden said, "and grateful."

She bowed her head while her husband asked the blessing.

Jim and Honey rode Jupiter and Lady down to the farm after dinner. They brought the news that Mr. Wheeler would, indeed, be glad to take Janie and Honey and Trixie, *and* Bobby, to Lakeside; it would only take part of the day.

"We'll leave at eleven and get to the airport in

Illinois around two o'clock," Honey said. "Mother called the Merediths to tell them."

"We'll be ready," Trixie said. "Oh, Honey, I'm so sure—so very sure."

When Trixie went to bed and the house quieted down, she couldn't sleep. There were so many things to think about, all of them seemingly unrelated, starting with the ride the Bob-Whites took through the woods, their talk with the men working at the marsh, and the furtive actions of the man they saw there; then the letter in answer to Trixie's letter to The Hague, the strange trip to the Bronx, what happened to their car there, and that smelly pipe—Trixie shivered as the odor came back to her. Then there was Janie's accident on Glen Road and her loss of memory; and Juliana's contradictory behavior, one time pleasant and attractive, and another time so strange and aloof—even cross.

"Instead of one mystery, Honey and I have several to solve," Trixie thought.

Time passed. Still Trixie tossed from side to side.

"I'll go down and get some milk," she said to herself and slipped into her robe and slippers.

In the kitchen a faint light burned. Janie was sitting there, her head resting on her arm.

"I didn't hear you," she told Trixie, startled. "I just couldn't sleep. I tried and tried and tried. So many things were rushing through my mind.

Mostly when I can't sleep it's because I'm frightened, not knowing who I am and trying to grope my way back."

Trixie put some milk into a pan to warm, then sat down next to Janie. "I'm so sorry."

"Don't be. This time I can't sleep because I'm so excited and happy. Just think, Trixie, I know now that I have a sister, and I'm going to see her tomorrow."

Trixie filled their glasses with hot milk.

"This ought to help us both go to sleep. I couldn't even close my eyes, for the same reason. I kept thinking how I'd feel if I were you."

Reddy, always alert to any sound, padded downstairs. He found a place on the floor between the two girls.

Janie smiled at the puzzlement in his brown eyes, which turned first to her and then to Trixie. She reached down to stroke his head lovingly.

"I feel as if I must have a dog of my own, somewhere," she said drowsily.

The clock on the shelf ticked contentedly. Outside, an owl hooted, and in the distance a dog barked. Reddy pricked up his ears.

Trixie opened the kitchen door and let him out. Then she said to Janie, "You'll find out about your own dog tomorrow—and probably a lot of other things."

Flight to Disappointment · 10

IN THE MORNING the big cozy kitchen buzzed with activity. Everyone seemed to be talking at once. Awkward, clumsy Reddy ran wildly up and down the stairs, trying to find out what the excitement was all about.

Much to her surprise but decidedly to her liking, Trixie found herself something of a heroine in her brothers' eyes. They thought she was pretty smart to go through the newspaper files in the library and said so. Even Mart, who usually added a few thistles to any bouquet he handed Trixie, jumped to her bidding and helped her set the table.

Janie, a yellow apron tied over the blue linen

dress she would wear on the plane, helped Mrs.
Belden turn the steaming pancakes.

Mr. Belden had gone to his work at the bank.
There was an extra spring to his step as he told his
family good-bye for the day and went out to his
car. In the short time Janie had been with them, he,
too, had grown fond of her. Now, though he hated
to have her leave, he was happy in the knowledge
that she would soon be with her own family.

Now she'll be "Barbara," Trixie thought, looking
at the other girl, where she stood at the stove.
She'll always be "Janie" to me.

"Don't you think it would be a good idea if you
telephoned Juliana and told her what has happened
and where you're going?" Mrs. Belden asked
Trixie.

Brian whistled. "Doesn't she know?"

"No, I forgot," Trixie answered. "Jeepers, we
should have told her. Maybe she'll want to go to the
airport with us. I think there'll be room in the station wagon."

"There's always room," Mart said. "Gol, I'll bet
Janie'll hate to leave our Bob-White bus."

"I'll bet she will, too," Janie herself said, "and
Crabapple Farm and every one of the Beldens,
but. . . ."

"You want to go to your own family, I know,"
Trixie said quickly. Then she dialed Mrs. Vanderpoel's number.

Juliana answered. Trixie told her the news about Janie and that Mr. Wheeler was going to fly her to Illinois.

"Jim isn't going on the plane, too, is he?" Juliana asked. The frantic note in her voice puzzled Trixie.

"No. It's only a small plane. Anyway, Regan's on the warpath about exercising the horses. He says they'll never be ready for the show if they aren't trained. Jim and Brian and Mart plan to jump them this afternoon."

"Heavens, the show isn't until November, is it?"

Everyone in the kitchen heard Juliana's voice. It was so high and shrill that Trixie had to hold the receiver away from her ear. "Does Jim have to take Jupiter out today? I want him to help me send another letter to Holland."

"Another? When did you decide that? Why all the hurry? They'll answer your letter soon."

"I don't want to wait any longer for those slow-pokes in Holland. Anyway, it's my business."

Trixie's reply showed the exasperation she felt. "You may *have* to wait for Jim to help you. One thing is sure. He and my brothers are going to take Jim's mother and father and all of us to the airport, where Mr. Wheeler will take off. Tom, their chauffeur, is sick. Then, after that, he'll have to ride the horses."

"He'll just *have* to help me. That's the most important thing!" Juliana shrilled.

Mart held his ears and Reddy began to bark.

"Then you ask him yourself and see what he can do."

Trixie hung up the receiver.

"You didn't sound very polite," her mother said.

"Well, she makes me furious," Trixie sputtered. "She never once asked anything about Janie's family—not once!"

Mrs. Belden filled the plates with steaming hot cakes, called to Bobby, then said quietly to Trixie, "I seem to remember a few times when you could think of only one problem at a time."

"If I ever get to be that selfish—oh, Moms," Trixie answered, "she's not a bit like Jim's cousin should be!"

"I think we're all high-strung this morning," Mrs. Belden said and put her arm around Trixie. "Have you helped Bobby find clean clothes to wear on the plane?"

"I have. He's putting a lot of things in that flight bag Dad brought him. You'd think he was going around the world."

"He's only been on a plane once before," Mart said. "He keeps saying Mr. Wheeler's plane is a jet fighter."

"It won't hurt you to help Bobby pretend," his mother answered. "More pancakes, anyone? Where did Janie go?"

"To finish packing her things."

"She didn't eat enough. There'll be no food on the plane, you know."

"Trust Miss Trask to send some along," Trixie said confidently. "Janie's too excited to eat. I get butterflies in my stomach every time I think of flying."

"You? Butterflies in your stomach over anything?" Mart whooped.

"Well, I do. Maybe I don't show it. No wonder Janie is nervous. Relatives she can't remember will be waiting at that airport in Illinois."

It was ten o'clock when Jim stopped the Bob-White station wagon in the driveway at Crabapple Farm. Patch, Jim's springer, had raced after the station wagon and stood panting, waiting for the car door to open. When it did, both dogs jumped in, tails wagging, trying to lick everyone in sight.

"Out!" Jim ordered. "Mrs. Belden, do you think you could keep Patch shut up somewhere till I come back?"

Mrs. Belden had come out of the house, drying her hands on her apron. "Of course I can, Jim." She turned to Honey's father and mother. "You haven't met Janie," she said, presenting the tall, gentle girl. "She has wanted especially to meet you," she told Mrs. Wheeler.

"I wanted to thank you for the pretty clothes you gave me through Miss Trask—" Janie began.

"Shhhh!" Mrs. Wheeler answered, taking Janie's

hands in hers. "Things have been happening to you pretty fast, haven't they?"

"Nice things," Janie said, "ever since I met the Bob-Whites and their families. Now Trixie and Honey have found my own family, I hope. And you and Mr. Wheeler are going to take me to them. I can hardly wait— I mean—well, I hate to leave everyone who has been so good to me."

"You were thinking, then, we ought to beat you?" Mart asked, and everyone laughed, breaking the tension.

At the airport, Bob, Mr. Wheeler's big, jovial pilot, had wheeled the plane into readiness. "Is this gang all going?" he asked anxiously. "I don't think there's quite enough room."

Mr. Wheeler laughed. "Don't worry, Bob. Jim, Brian, and Mart have just come to wave us off. Do you mind if Bobby sits with you? He wants to help spot enemy planes."

"Climb right in, Ace," Bob told the little boy. "Do you have your telescope ready?"

Quietly, Trixie asked Jim, "Did Juliana talk to you this morning?"

"Yes, she did." Jim's freckled face sobered. "I feel sorry for her. She's missing most of that vacation she expected to have in the Poconos. She gets terribly nervous, just sitting around waiting. She wants to send off another letter to Holland, for immediate answer. I'll help her when I get back."

Jim's so good, Trixie thought to herself. *I'm ashamed when I'm so hateful. It's a wonder he ever puts up with me. I didn't have to say what I did to Juliana. Maybe Moms is right—that I hate to share any of the Bob-Whites with anyone else. To be real honest, I hate particularly to share Jim. He's so special. I guess I expected his cousin to be special, too.* Trixie's eyes grew wistful. *More like Janie . . . maybe.*

"Hey, Trixie, are you with us?" Bob shouted. "In you go. *And* off you go!" he told Jim, Brian, and Mart. "You're supposed to have scrammed off this field minutes ago. You can watch from the airport deck."

The propellers spun. The passengers settled in their seats. The engine roared. There was a rush of wind, and they were airborne.

Bobby, all eyes and ears, whitened a little as the plane gained altitude but sat bravely alert till the ship leveled off and the roar subsided to a pleasant hum.

Down below, familiar buildings blurred, then finally disappeared when a floor of fluffy white clouds obscured the view.

Trixie and Honey kept up a constant chatter, leaning forward now and then to speak to Janie, who sat with Mrs. Wheeler in the seat in front of them. Mostly, Trixie thought, they were all talking to keep Janie from having any time to think.

As Trixie had thought, Miss Trask had provided
a hamper of food. Honey found it, at her mother's
request, and passed around chicken sandwiches,
apples, cookies, popcorn, and small cartons of milk
with straws.

Bobby spilled popcorn all over the floor, then
puckered his face, expecting to be scolded, and
scrambled around trying to pick it up.

"Forget it, Bobby," Mr. Wheeler told him.
"There's plenty more. Just ask Honey for some."

Even as Mr. Wheeler spoke the plane began to
lose altitude, and Trixie guessed they were near-
ing the Illinois airport.

Janie's face had lost its high color. She gazed
down from the window, drew her head back,
looked around at her friends in the plane, then
peered down again at the earth, which was coming
closer all the time.

"It's easy to see how jittery she is," Trixie
thought.

When the plane bumped on the runway and
taxied to a stop, Janie held back. When the doors
opened and the stairway came up, Bob, the pilot,
led Bobby out first. They had landed at a part of
the field reserved for private planes, so Janie's or-
deal of meeting her family was postponed. A waiting jeep swept them all up and took them to the airport gate.

Inside the long corridor, Trixie walked on one

side of Janie, Honey on the other. Then, as the waiting crowd beyond the rope grew nearer, the girls each put an arm around Janie's waist. Their eyes darted here and there, trying to seek out someone who could be Janie's sister. They expected to hear a glad cry at any moment.

People met people, then disappeared to cars or taxis. The oncoming crowd melted into the great surging mass inside the huge waiting room.

A woman, standing apart, looked in their direction and waved wildly. Trixie, Honey, and Janie waved back. Trixie watched the woman's eyes on Janie, waiting to see recognition in the face so bright with anticipation. The woman came nearer and nearer. Her husband waved his hat in greeting, and they both passed by to be swept into the arms of a middle-aged couple just behind Janie.

"It wasn't anyone who knew me," Janie's voice was low, sick with disappointment. Mr. and Mrs. Wheeler, Trixie, and Honey exchanged glances of sympathetic frustration.

"I'll bet that's Janie's sister over by the big window," Bobby cried. "See, Trixie?"

A young woman watching, shading her eyes with her cupped hands, turned eagerly. "Trixie? Did someone say 'Trixie'?"

"Yes!" Trixie cried eagerly. "Are you Mrs. Meredith, Janie's—I mean, Barbara's sister?"

"Yes, I am," the young woman said, her face

anxious and inquiring. "Didn't Barbara come with you? Was she too sick?"

Janie, with a low moan, dropped down on a waiting-room bench, her voice despairing. "Then I'm not Barbara."

"Oh, you aren't my sister," Mrs. Meredith cried. "Oh, Tom." She turned to her husband, deep disappointment in her voice. "This girl isn't Barbara at all. Where *is* Barbara?"

Janie moaned. "I'm still *nobody*."

Trixie felt the bottom fall out of her stomach. She had been *so* sure.

Barbara's sister turned to Janie. "You can't be 'nobody'—not with friends like yours. They'll help you find your family someday. You *are* alive." Her voice filled with anguish. "*I don't even know whether my sister is alive or not.*"

She started to cry, and her husband, with a quick word of thanks, led his wife away.

Bobby, unable to understand what had been going on and upset by what he saw, began to cry, too. It had been such fun up until now.

Janie instantly forgot herself in her concern for Mrs. Meredith and for the little boy in his panic. She pulled Bobby close to comfort him. "See that newsstand right over there?" She pointed. "They have ice-cream cones over there—big ones, all colors, double ones—for little boys. Shall we see if we can find one?"

Mrs. Wheeler clicked her tongue in amazement at the girl's courage in the face of such bitter disappointment.

Trixie and Honey just stood, wordless.

"Well, what's keeping us from those cones?" Mr. Wheeler asked heartily and lifted Bobby to his shoulder as they crossed the great width of the waiting room and lined up at the ice cream bar.

It was Janie who kept up everybody's spirits all the way home. It was Janie who thought of gay riddles for Bobby to guess. It was Janie, joined by Bob, the pilot, who hummed familiar tunes and had everyone singing.

As the plane came closer to the green trees of New York State, however, and the Hudson spread its silvery brown ribbon far below them, they all became quiet.

Down there Jim, Brian, and Mart—quite probably Mr. and Mrs. Belden, too—would be watching for a speck in the sky. They would be waiting for the glad details of Janie's happy reunion with her family.

Trixie saw the shadow cross Janie's face, saw her draw herself in tensely, as if preparing herself for still another cruel blow. Then she fell behind the others as the party left the plane.

Someone else—not she—would have to announce the bad news.

Mystery Car at the Treasure Hunt · 11

THE BOB-WHITES of the Glen had gathered at their clubhouse to tell Diana and Dan what had occurred the day before. Too, they wanted to discuss the problem with all the members present, to see if they could figure out what to do next.

"The one thing about this business of Janie that I never can understand," said Dan, "is that everyone who has ever met her likes her, so—"

"That's true," Trixie interrupted. "It was true at the hospital, with all the nurses, and the first thing all the other Candy Stripers ask us when we go to the hospital is 'How's Janie?' "

"That's what I mean," Dan went on. There was a

frown on his deep-tanned face. "So why hasn't there been just one little inquiry from somewhere about a girl like her, who must have turned up missing?"

"It's a mystery, for sure," Trixie said. "Don't think it doesn't worry Janie. We told you how marvelous she was on the plane coming home."

"Yeah, and all of it put on." Mart sat down at the clubhouse table on the bench next to Trixie. "Why don't you just work on Janie's identity, instead of wasting time worrying over 'mysterious' calls about Jim's aunt, and a 'mysterious' man at the marsh, and a 'mysterious' guy who jimmied up our car in the Bronx and left a 'mysterious' pipe?"

"If you'll just give me time—" Trixie began.

"If all of us do give you time, you'll find out who Janie is. I know you will," Honey said loyally. "You may make some mistakes, but you'll find out eventually. I'm going to help you every way I can."

"Gosh, so are we," Mart said quickly. "I just wish she'd concentrate on Janie."

"How do you know I'm not?" Trixie asked with spirit. "You're not a detective, Mart, and you don't know how to recognize clues when you see them or how to sense the way the wind blows."

"I know this much: It's blowing up a storm for Janie just now, and not even the Belden-Wheeler Detective Agency is protecting her from it."

"We're trying, Mart Belden," Honey said. "Why

don't you come up with one of your marvelous ideas?"

"Sarcasm ill becomes you," Mart said loftily. "Anyway, if I don't do anything, I don't keep making mistakes."

"Heaven knows I don't want to make any more mistakes," Trixie said sadly. "When I saw that bewildered look come over Janie's face when Mrs. Meredith didn't recognize her, and when I realize how brave she's been. . . ."

"That's the worst thing about amnesia," Brian, the future doctor, said. "I never knew anything about loss of memory till that day Trixie and Honey came home from the hospital and told us about Janie. Since then, I've been reading up on it. There doesn't seem to be a lot anyone can do."

"You were saying, 'That's the worst thing about amnesia,'" Honey said. "What is, Brian?"

"The fact that some contact with the person's past is necessary to stimulate his memory. Then, in a flash, it all comes back. We just don't seem to be able to dig up that trigger. I was so sure you'd bring back good news yesterday."

"I wouldn't go through that experience again for anything," Trixie said. "Next time I'll be sure."

Jim broke in quietly, "If anyone asks me, and they haven't, I think it would help Janie a lot, and us, too, if we'd think up some fun for her."

"Shake!" Mart said, extending his hand. "You

sound more like a doctor than Brian. Now, what will we do, and when?"

"Why not a barbecue tonight?" Dan suggested.

"At our house!" Trixie cried. "A surprise one, for Janie."

"With a treasure hunt," Honey said.

"Maybe Janie's too old for a treasure hunt," Diana suggested, but she was hooted down by the others.

"Janie may be past twenty, but she sure doesn't look it. She likes everything we do, too," Trixie insisted. Then her face fell. "What chance would we have for a surprise party with Bobby. . . ."

"He's a darling," Honey said, "but I know what you mean. Just try to keep a secret around him."

"Well," Mart said, "how could we have a surprise for Janie, anyway, when she's right there all the time?"

"Miss Trask is the answer," Jim said. "If Honey and I ask her, she'll figure out some sort of expedition today that will include Bobby *and* Janie. Let's see—" He looked at his wristwatch. "It's past twelve o'clock now. You beat it home for lunch, all of you, and about one fifteen, see if Miss Trask doesn't show up at Crabapple Farm."

It was one fifteen on the dot when Miss Trask did, indeed, show up.

Bobby was ecstatic, for, next to Old Brom, Miss

Trask was his favorite "best friend." "We're going to the zoo," he cried. "They have a new baby elephant there."

Janie, invited, went along.

Reddy, uninvited, went along, too, his tail a semaphore, his whole body wagging happily.

As the car disappeared down Glen Road, Trixie drew a little notebook from her pocket. "Now, food first. We'll get it at Mr. Lytell's grocery. Miss Trask always wants us to buy all the groceries we can from him."

"Yeah." Mart grinned. "I think she and Mr. Lytell are sorta—"

"Of course they like one another," Honey said, bristling, "and they have for a long time. What of it?"

"Not a thing. Not a thing," Mart said airily. "If she doesn't mind how cranky he gets and thinks he's the Apollo Belvedere, it's okay with me. I say it's okay."

"Boy, I'll never forget how he was so patient with me when I wanted to buy my jalopy," Brian said.

"Mr. Lytell is an oddball," Mart said, tongue in cheek, "but he's all heart. He's all heart!"

Trixie wrote "hamburger" and repeated it out loud. Then she went on. "Pickles. Potato Chips. Lemonade mix."

"Cokes!" Mart said. "Say, why do we buy all this

stuff? Moms always has the freezer full of hamburger, don't you, Moms?"

"Of course I do," Mrs. Belden said as she came
into the kitchen. "I'll fix a salad and bake a cake.
Anyone want baked beans?"

"Nix on the hamburger," Jim said, "and pickles,
potato chips, and other stuff. This is a Bob-White
party, and we'll use our funds. It's okay on the
cake, though, Mrs. Belden."

"I'll fix the salad, too, and the baked beans,"
Mrs. Belden said, laughing. "You'll want to invite
Juliana, won't you?"

"Sure!" Brian said heartily. "We'll stop at Mrs.
Vanderpoel's house when we go to the store. I sure
hope she's heard something from Holland."

When they stopped, Juliana said yes, she'd love
to go to the party, and no, she hadn't heard anything from The Hague. "Time's getting shorter and
shorter, too." Her voice sharpened.

"Oh, well, don't fret," Mrs. Vanderpoel told her.
"It'll come in time for you to join your friends, I
know. I wish there was something I could send for
the party. There're cookies, of course. Janie does
like my cookies. I'll send some with Juliana when
she goes."

"Where next?" Jim asked as he backed out of the
drive.

"The record shop," Mart said. "There's one I've
got to have. The Kelpies—they're English. They

have a flamenco guitarist who's something."

"We want dance records, mostly," Trixie said. "Just who dances the flamenco? Oh, figure that one out yourself. Honey and Di and I have to list the treasures to be found in the hunt. Let's have suggestions."

" 'Eye of newt' and 'toe of frog,' " Mart sang out.

" 'Wool of bat' and 'tongue of dog,' " Jim put in.

Laughter from the backseat rewarded them as the car moved on to Sleepyside.

"If it's that good!" Mart snorted.

"It is!" Honey insisted as Trixie added "candy wrapper" to a growing list: light bulb, horseshoe, fresh egg, yellow rose, old glove, five green mulberries, apple core, dog bone.

At a little after six, Miss Trask let Bobby and Janie out at the drive, with Reddy bounding after them.

"I heard a record going way down the road!" Bobby cried. Then the little boy's eyes grew big as he glanced from lanterns to red-checked cloth on the picnic table. "Who's having a party?"

"Surprise for Janie!" the Bob-Whites called.

They joined hands with Juliana in a circle around her. "Surprise for Janie!"

Janie, confused for a moment, suddenly clapped her hands, eyes dancing. "This is fun!"

"You stay, too, won't you, Miss Trask?" Trixie asked.

The slender, gray-haired woman demurred, then, as the boys shouted, "Yeah, Miss Trask! Yeah, Miss Trask!" she weakened and busied herself helping Mrs. Belden in the kitchen.

It wasn't long till Mr. Belden called from the barbecue, "Soup's on!" and there was a rush for the picnic table.

The mound of hamburgers disappeared to the accompaniment of laughter, jokes, and teasing. Casseroles were scraped to the last bite, and cake and cookies disappeared.

The sun dropped in the western sky. Even Reddy stopped begging for handouts; and the Bob-Whites and their guests, groaning, pushed back from the table.

The treasure hunt started. Brian, the leader, read off the list of treasures. "Everyone is to go by himself—no teamwork. The first one back with the whole list—the entire list—gets a pocket transistor, gift of Diana's father, and it's a honey. Now, scram!"

"Reddy goes with me," Bobby said. "I know where every one of those things is . . . I think. Janie, you go round the barn that way. The mulberry tree's there. Juliana, you go through the orchard and you'll get an apple core. Want me to tell you more?"

"Just find your own treasures, Bobby. It'll keep

you busy enough," Brian said as he disappeared into the shrubbery.

The big boys raced up Glen Road. On the vast Wheeler estate, they were bound to find the treasures in record time.

For a while all was quiet, except for the sound of quick running feet, an occasional shout of triumph, or the distant barking of a dog.

Trixie, in her mother's garden to add the yellow rose to her collection, heard a car stop on the road below her home. *That's funny,* thought Trixie, instantly alert. *Why would a car stop on this stretch of Glen Road? No houses, except the ruins of Ten Acres. If they were our visitors, they'd use our driveway. I wonder....* Then, with a mental shrug, she turned back to the roses. Suddenly she heard Reddy's sharp bark, closely followed by Bobby's frightened cry: "Trixie!"

For a split second, she froze; then she darted toward the house.

Immediately Bob-Whites, running from every direction, converged on the patio.

Trixie was the first to reach Bobby.

"I dropped my sack with my treasures," he howled. "And I broked my egg!" He held up a dripping paper bag. "It's awful sticky."

Reddy growled low in his throat.

"What happened to make you call for Trixie?" his father asked.

"It was that man . . . that man in a car. . . ."

"I heard a car stop down the road," Trixie said. "What did the man do?" she asked Bobby.

"He had a growly voice," Bobby said. "Worse than Reddy's, 'n he said . . . he said—"

"Yes. Go on!" his father prodded.

"He said did I know where Mrs. Vanderpoel lived," Bobby whimpered.

"Is that all, for pete's sake?" Mart asked.

"Did you tell the man where she lived?" Mrs. Belden asked. "Brian, you and Jim go and see if the car is still there. It does seem to me a simple question to ask."

"What did I say about the Belden family making a big production over nothing?" Mart asked when the other boys came back and reported no car on Glen Road.

"It's not . . . exactly . . . nothing," Trixie said thoughtfully. "It's a little odd."

"What's odd about a man asking a simple direction?" Mart asked.

"Just this," Trixie answered. "All the lights were on at our house. If he really wanted to know where Mrs. Vanderpoel lived, why didn't he stop here and ask?"

"Maybe that's just the reason. Maybe he thought it was a party," Mart said. "Maybe he didn't want to get out of his car when a dog growled at him. Maybe half a dozen things. One sure thing, there was nothing mysterious about it, Trixie. The treasure hunt is all shot now. I vote we give the transistor radio to Janie."

"To remember the treasure hunt that didn't click." Honey giggled. "I'd like her to have it, anyway."

"Yeah! Yeah! Yeah!" the Bob-Whites agreed. Miss Trask placed the radio in Janie's lap. Janie, protesting but delighted, examined the little set enthusiastically.

"How about getting your guitar, Mart?" Diana begged. "We can have a hootenanny all our own. Didn't you say Janie taught you an English ballad? Will you sing it for us, Janie? Is everyone here?"

Trixie gazed around the picnic table, where they had all gathered. "Where's Juliana?"

"She went through the apple orchard, where I told her," Bobby said. "I thought she could get the apple core there. There she comes now."

"Why all the excitement?" Jim's cousin asked, dropping down on the bench near him. "All I found was an apple. Maybe Bobby will eat it down to the core for me."

"Didn't you hear him yelling?" Mart asked, and handed his guitar to Janie. "He broke up the treasure hunt."

"It was someone asking the way to Mrs. Vanderpoel's house. It was nothing. Bobby got a little excited," Brian said.

"All that fuss about someone asking a direction?" Juliana asked. "It doesn't take much to upset Bobby."

"*Do* sing your song, Janie. Mart said it was a lovely ballad," Trixie urged. She thought, *If you knew it was "all that fuss," you must have heard it. Did you hear it and pretend you didn't? If so, why? It's odd, no matter what Mart says.*

Janie twanged a few chords and in a low voice sang plaintively:

"In Camelot, where Arthur died,
    The mist hangs low and cold.
In fading light, Round Table Knights
    Are ghosts, who once were bold.
For nothing's left of that dear age
    Of grace and chivalry,
Save wild wind racing through the crags
    In mournful threnody.
      Alas!
The wild wind races through the crags
    In mournful threnody."

"Ugh! That's not only sad; it's grisly, too," Juliana said, shuddering.

"Most English ballads are sad. They run to minor chords. They're neat!" Mart said.

"Maybe English ballads have to be sad," Juliana insisted, "but for a 'cheer-up' party. . . ."

"She has a point there," Jim agreed. "Mart, how

about that Catskill song we sang on the towboat on
the Mississippi?"

"Okay, if you'll all sing along." Mart ran through
a verse of chords, then sang out lustily:

"We'll sing you a song of the Catskills, oh,
   A song of the mountain men, oh.

"Rip Van Winkle, on a stormy night,
   Left his wife and went up to the height
   Of the Catskill range, where Hudson's men
   Played ninepins merrily, but when
   They gave him a drink, he drank so deep
   It sent him into a twenty-year sleep.

"We'll sing you a song of the Catskills, oh,
   A song of the mountain men, oh.

"When Rip awakened, he yawned and said,
   'Twenty years?' then rubbed his head,
   Took up his stick and called his dog,
   Set off for town in the morning fog,

Singing:

" 'Now, many a man's been twenty years wed,
   And many a man's been twenty years dead,
   I'll take the second, you take the first,
   Of all man's troubles, a wife's the worst.'

"We've sung you a song of the Catskills, oh,
   A song of the mountain men, oh."

"All together, now," Brian said, clapping and laughing, "another chorus!"

"We've sung you a song of the Catskills, oh,
A song of the mountain men, oh."

Trixie, swinging her arms in rhythm, noticed suddenly that Janie wasn't singing with them, not even humming the tune. A strange expression had crept over her face.

"Play it again, please!" Janie begged Mart when the singing had stopped. "It almost seemed . . . it was when I was in college. . . ."

Juliana jumped to her feet. "It's all too utterly morbid! Gruesome! I'm going home. I had no idea of the time. Cousin Jim, will you take me to Mrs. Vanderpoel's house?"

She's done it again, Trixie thought. *She's broken the spell. Why does she always interrupt when Janie is about to remember? Does she do it on purpose? That's too fantastic! But—*

Jim left with Juliana.

Mart put some dance records on the player.

"Dibs on dancing with Janie!" Brian shouted and swung her out into the center of the patio.

Soon Mart and Diana and Trixie and Dan followed, arms and legs flying, shouting to the beat and melody as the disk whirled. Reddy, yipping joyfully, ran in and out among the dancers, Bobby in close pursuit.

The frenzy and tempo increased as record followed record.

Where can Jim be? Trixie thought. *What's keeping him so long?*

As though in answer to her question, the lights of the station wagon shone across the patio.

Jim came running across the lawn, and the dancing stopped.

"A car was parked at Mrs. Vanderpoel's when I got there," he burst out. "A green Buick."

"That was the growly man who told me where did Mrs. Vanderpoel live," Bobby said.

"Who was it?" Trixie asked.

"You can search me. I was going to walk to the house with Juliana, but she closed the car door before I could get out and told me not to bother. I watched through the window. All I could see was a man sitting in the car. I couldn't tell who he was—probably wouldn't know, anyway. Then—get this—Juliana didn't go into Mrs. Vanderpoel's house at all. She got in that car! She drove off with that guy. The whole thing seemed kooky to me."

"Aha!" Mart said, twirling an imaginary moustache. "So you are seeing mysteries, too!"

Jim didn't answer Mart. "All I can say," he said, "is that I wish Spider Webster still lived at Mrs. Vanderpoel's house. He'd know if something funny was going on."

"Yeah," Brian said, "Sergeant Molinson wasn't

thinking straight when he let Spider leave the Sleepyside police force . . . even if he would have had to raise his salary."

"He was a friend to the Bob-Whites, all right, when we were in the jam with the thieves who tried to steal our antiques at the show." Trixie sighed. "We could use him now."

"You can say that again," Dan agreed. "He didn't think we were imagining things, especially Trixie and Honey, the way Sergeant Molinson does."

"Yeah," Jim said. "You'd think he'd learn sometime, wouldn't you? The number of times Trixie has solved his cases for him!"

The Warning Signs Are Gone! • 12

Moms, where's Janie?"

Trixie, in her Candy Striper uniform, came racing down the stairs.

Mrs. Belden put a sheet of cookies in the oven, closed the door, and answered, "I *do* wish you wouldn't run everyplace, Trixie. Can't you ever walk down the stairs?"

"I'll try. But where's Janie? Look at the time . . . almost one o'clock. Jim and Honey will stop by for me in a minute. He's taking us to the hospital today, because the brake on Honey's bike has to be fixed. Where is Janie, Moms?"

"I don't ask Janie to register in and out, dear. I

imagine she's in the garden. Or have you looked in her room?"

"I just called down the hall. Didn't you hear me? We'll be late at the hospital if she doesn't show up. If we're late we'll get demerits and spoil everything. She's supposed to be here."

"Why is Janie supposed to be here now?"

"She wanted to go to the hospital with us, to visit with the nurses and maybe Dr. Gregory. It was the last thing she said last night. I haven't even seen her since breakfast, have you?"

"Yes . . . let me think . . . she wanted to help me with the baking, and I told her I had almost finished, and then—dear me, Trixie, I don't remember what she said then. I think she said she was going to take a walk. She spends a lot of time in the woods. Just be a little patient; she'll be here."

"She'd better hurry. Jim and Honey are stopping the station wagon out there right now. She's forgotten, that's what. She's forgotten all about it. Oh, well, she'll have to go with us another day. 'Bye, Moms." At the door Trixie met Honey coming in. "Why, Honey, what's the matter?"

Honey threw herself down on a chair in the kitchen.

"Jim has me worried, and I'd like to hear what your mom thinks about it. He says he shouldn't have left Juliana last night till he was sure she was safe in the house. He didn't like that business of

that green Buick out in front of Mrs. Vanderpoel's
house. He didn't like it at all. He says he should
have found out who it was."

"Oh, Juliana probably had a date with someone.
She's over twenty-one. Why was he so bothered?
What did he do about it?" said Mrs. Belden.

"This morning he went over to Mrs. Vanderpoel's. He wanted to make sure Juliana was all
right. She *is* his cousin, after all. And she doesn't
have any friends in Sleepyside—at least, we didn't
think she had."

"What do you mean?"

"Just this: Juliana wasn't home, and it wasn't
even nine o'clock in the morning. Mrs. Vanderpoel
said she had gone out, that someone had called her
and she left."

"Was it a man or a woman?"

"That's what Jim asked, and Mrs. Vanderpoel
said she didn't know, because Juliana answered the
telephone. I don't think we need to worry about
any lack of friends for Juliana. Mrs. Vanderpoel
said she always gets to the telephone first to answer
it and that ninety-nine percent of the calls are for
her."

Trixie nodded her head. "Of course, she *is* awfully attractive, and she did live for a long time in
the Bronx. She probably knows a lot of people
there. It isn't so far away."

"That isn't all," Honey went on. "Mrs. Vanderpoel told Jim our party must have lasted pretty late last night, because Juliana still hadn't come home at one o'clock in the morning."

"Well, see? She went someplace with that man in the green Buick," Trixie said.

"I think I may have to remind you, Honey, of the same thing I spoke to Trixie about," Mrs. Belden said. "She's been worried because Janie isn't here to go to the hospital with you, and Jim is concerned about Juliana's actions. Both of these girls are over twenty-one, and I don't imagine they want anyone to monitor their movements. In a way, I think it's rather funny."

"What's funny?" Jim asked from the doorway. "I didn't know you were going to make a visit here, Honey. It's time we were moving. Say, what's so funny, Mrs. Belden?"

"The fact that ever since each one of you has passed from twelve to teen, Brian and Mart, too, your greatest obsession has been: 'Don't keep track of me every minute. I can take care of myself.' Now look at you. Juliana is somewhere going about her business, and Janie probably forgot it was Candy Striper day and went off into the woods. Sometimes she takes a sandwich and stays for hours. She loves the woods as much as we do, who were born right here.

"Just go ahead to the hospital, girls. From what Trixie said, too, Jim, Juliana left in a huff last night and probably wants to be left alone. I'm sure she's anxious for some word from Holland, so she can finish her business here and be off to join her friends."

"Okay, I guess you're right," Jim said sheepishly. "We aren't too consistent, are we? If *you* were in a thing about Trixie not showing up someplace, we'd think you were the prize worrywart. Okay, come on, kids."

It was after five o'clock when the girls came back from the hospital. They found Mrs. Belden really disturbed.

"Janie hasn't shown up yet," she said. "I should have paid more attention to your concern about her when she wasn't here to go to the hospital with you, Trixie."

"Was Bobby with her? She always takes him."

"Bobby wasn't with her." Mrs. Belden's strained voice showed her anxiety. "He's spending the day with Jerry and Larry Lynch."

At the sound of Bobby's name, Reddy barked sharply, startling Trixie. "Then *he* isn't with her, either." Trixie put her hand on the setter's red head. "Jim?" she said, looking expectantly at Honey's brother.

"Where are Brian and Mart?" he asked abruptly.

"I sent them off to the woods to look for Janie. I couldn't wait any longer. They just left. They haven't been gone long, and if you want to catch them, Jim, I think you can."

"I'll go, too," Trixie said quickly. "I'll get a flashlight."

"Me, too," Honey added. "There are other flashlights in the station wagon. I'll get them."

"Hurry," Mrs. Belden said. "If you're going, go now and at least catch up with Jim. It's better if you are with one of the boys."

"Keep Reddy here, please, Moms," Trixie called back to her mother. "We'd only have to spend half our time rounding him up."

Near Mr. Maypenny's house, the trio caught up with Brian and Mart. They were talking with Dan.

"I know the place she most always goes," Dan told them. "There's a stump there, and the grass is all tramped down. I've seen Janie sitting there reading a book. Follow me."

They set off on the well-worn trail, but when they reached the stump, there was no Janie.

A paperback book of Robert Frost's poems was there, though, opened and turned facedown. Janie's wristwatch was there, too, turned faceup.

"Honey," said Trixie shakily, "Janie *had* been watching the time! She *had* intended to be back to go to the hospital with us!" One of the poems was marked. As Trixie read the last line, "And miles to go before I sleep," fear tightened its fingers around her heart.

Just past the place where Janie had rested, the trail narrowed and circled, leading to the top, high above the river. Shafts of pinkish light from the lowering sun outlined the tall, rough trunks of rugged pines. Their rustling green needles in the eerie quiet sent chills up Trixie's spine.

Nobody spoke a word. Dan led the way, and Brian, Mart, Trixie, Honey, and Jim followed.

From time to time one of them broke the silence to call out sharply, "Janie! Janie! Janie!"

"She may have lost her way," Dan said, whispering as one does when fearful and worried. "You go that way, Mart, you and Brian and Honey. Hunt for her back farther in the woods. Keep calling! We'll go this way, Jim and Trixie and I. Farther along, the two paths come together."

"Aren't they liable to get lost themselves?" Trixie asked as they separated.

"They can't," Dan said. "They'll see the signs."

The signs! At a sudden realization, Trixie's heart almost stopped beating. *There aren't any signs anywhere!*

Dan and Jim had spurted ahead.

"Dan!" Trixie screamed. "Jim!" The boys stopped. "The warning signs! They aren't here!" Trixie cried. "Janie couldn't have seen them. She wouldn't have known that the ground breaks away at the edge of the cliff. And you won't be any good to anyone if you go diving over the cliff."

"She's right," Dan said. "Beyond here that layer of earth is so thin that we'd just go down, head over heels."

"But we *have* to look over that edge somehow," Jim insisted. "Janie may be down there and hurt."

"Have you found her?" Mart called, bursting through the undergrowth where the two paths came together.

"What's the matter with everyone?" Honey, following Mart, asked in a shaking voice.

"The signs have been taken away," Trixie groaned. "Janie didn't know. She didn't know!"

"The first thing to do," Dan said quietly, "is to climb down the trail here—the one we use to go to the marsh. Trixie, you and Honey stay here and keep calling."

Dan knows every inch of this forest, Trixie said to herself. *We must trust him . . . do as he says.*

"Down at the bottom of the bluff," Dan called back as he followed the other boys, "we'll know more than we do now." His voice broke off.

Trixie moaned. "He means they *may* find Janie. I don't believe she's down there! Let's keep on calling her."

Desperately and frantically, the girls' voices rose. "Janie, Janie! Janie! Where are you, Janie? Janie! Janie!"

After what seemed hours, the boys came scrambling back, their faces grim.

"We didn't find Janie," Dan said. "We did find something else."

"The signs!" Mart exploded. "The warning signs, in a heap, all smashed to pieces!"

Trixie gasped, stifling a cry of terror.

"They must have been thrown from the cliff," Brian said, "deliberately. When we find whoever did it—"

"That's for later," Jim said. His voice, quiet and reassuring, comforted Trixie. He went on. "We didn't find Janie down there. That's something for us to think about. Dan, you've got your hunting lantern with you. We're going to need it, all right. We've only begun our search!"

Dan fastened the lantern to his shoulder. Its powerful beam cut through the fast-gathering mist curling up from the river.

"Come with me, Jim," he said. "We'll crawl along well back from the cliff's edge. If there's a broken place there, it may be where Janie could have slipped. If she did, she may have caught on something on the cliffside, beyond the reach of our voices."

"She may not be able to answer, even if she hears our voices," said Trixie, on the verge of tears.

"We'll have to shine the light over the edge and try to locate her," Dan said.

Quickly Trixie stepped between Dan and Jim. "Let me go," she begged. "I'm so much lighter. I can crawl closer and see more."

Jim started to speak, but with a rush of words Trixie stopped him. "*Please!* You can hold tight to my feet, both of you. There isn't the slightest danger, not with you both holding on to me."

Fifty feet beyond the path to the marsh, Dan paused, unhooked his light, and swung it up and down along the rim of the bluff. Trixie, shading her eyes, followed the movement of the beam till Dan, with a sigh, sank to one knee and said, "In a half a dozen places all along that cliff, the edge has broken off. Someone could have gone over. It's almost dark, and I don't know what to do next. Nobody is *sure* Janie came this far. No one is sure that she even came into the woods."

"*I* am," Trixie said firmly. "We found her book and her watch! Janie said once she wanted to explore every inch of these woods. She must have started exploring. If she didn't see a warning sign, she might have walked along that ledge. She— Let's call her again." Trixie's voice rose. "Janie! Janie!"

They all listened. There was no answer.

"Janie!" the boys called, their voices loud and hoarse. "Janie! Janie! *Janie!*"

Again they listened, straining their ears.

Out of the stillness came a faint sound!

"Did you hear that?" Trixie cried.

Frantically she crawled forward, calling again and again, "Janie! Where are you? Janie!"

"Trixie! Watch out!" Jim shouted.

With one desperate gesture, he and Dan caught Trixie's feet and held them tight. "Have you gone crazy?" Jim asked, his voice frenzied.

"Let me go! It's Janie. She's down there. I heard her!"

Trixie tried to pull her feet free.

"I'm going closer. Listen!" she commanded. "Oh, please, *listen!* Janie! Answer me!"

From below, out of the blackness, there came a groan, faint—almost lost—but unmistakable.

"Did you hear that?" Trixie cried. "It's Janie. *She's alive!*"

Cupping her hands over her mouth, Trixie called, "Hold on tight, Janie! Hold on! We're here! We'll bring you up!"

Turning to Dan, she begged, "Give me the lantern, please. Hold tight to me now, both of you. I'll go closer . . . look over that edge . . . find where Janie is. . . ."

Trixie's Courage • 13

THE LANTERN sent its stream of light hunting around in the darkness below Trixie, down a sheer drop to the river's edge.

Here and there, dark clumps of scrub pine showed up, dark blobs against the rugged cliffside. But nothing else.

"Janie!" Trixie called over the edge of the precipice. "Janie, where are you?"

Faintly the answer came back. "Here, Trixie. Down . . . here."

Frantically Trixie swung the light into an arc, seeking, searching.

"Here!" Janie repeated weakly.

The light picked out a patch of Janie's blue dress, caught in a smudge of shrubbery.

"I've found her!" Trixie called back triumphantly. "Are you hurt, Janie?" She tried to keep the fear from her voice. "Can you move?"

"I don't . . . think . . . I'm hurt . . . much. Don't . . . worry, Trixie."

Trixie had to strain her ears to hear Janie's words. *Isn't it like Janie to tell me not to worry?* Trixie thought.

"We're coming!" Trixie shouted, with confidence she was far from feeling. "The boys and Honey are with me. Hold on!"

Slowly Trixie inched her way back from the edge, told the boys what she had seen, and asked helplessly, "How can we ever get her back up here?"

"Don't panic!" Jim answered. "We'll take care of it some way. The minute you crawled back, Dan took off for the woods. He knows where Mr. Maypenny keeps ropes and axes stored to use for felling trees. That's a break. He said it isn't far from here and he'd be back in a few minutes."

"Good! Where is everybody? Do they know that we've found Janie?"

"I thought Mart and Honey should go home and tell Dad," Brian said. "Maybe they'll call the sheriff."

"Of course, Brian," Trixie said. "But, in the

meantime, are we going to let Janie lie down there? She's been there for hours and hours. She said she doesn't think she's hurt badly. You know Janie, though. I hate to think of her lying down there one more minute."

"I know," Brian said. "But if she has broken bones, we can't even move her until help comes. What else can we do but wait?"

At that moment Dan returned with lengths of stout rope.

"If you don't know, I do," Trixie said firmly. "We can tie those ropes under my arms, and I can go over the edge as easy as anything. Then I can at least see how badly Janie's hurt and if we *can* move her."

"*You* can go?" Brian was scornful. "I think not, Trixie."

"Why can't I go? I'm the one who knows just where Janie is. I'm the one who weighs the least. I'm the one who can go right up to the edge without breaking it off. I showed you that. I'm the one—"

"You're the one who's going to stay right up here where you belong," Jim said. "I'll go. Give me the ropes, Dan."

He fastened the rope ends securely under his arms.

"Now, loop the other ends around those pine trees. Brian, you can make a running knot."

"I know how to make a slipknot, all right, but I'll tell you this, Jim: You'll never even get to the edge of that bluff. You're too heavy. We'll either have to wait till help comes or try to reach Janie from below someway."

"Climb up that sheer cliff?" Dan asked. "Are you crazy?"

Trixie, burning with frustration, cried out, "Nobody seems to remember that I went right to the edge and it held! Is there any good reason *why* I can't be the one to go down to Janie? Is there, Dan?"

"It's too dangerous. Don't say any more about it."

"It's not as dangerous for me as it would be for any one of you— Oh, look at Jim! He's on his way! Watch out!" she screamed. "Pull him back! Dan— Brian!"

In his haste, Jim had thrown his weight forward too fast. The earth loosened under him and began to fall away. Froglike, he drew his legs back to firmer ground. "If you hadn't been so determined to do it yourself, Trixie . . ." he sputtered.

"Oh, Jim, you can be so stubborn. Why can't you see that I'm the one to go down there? Maybe some of that dirt and stone fell on Janie. How can we possibly leave her there alone till Mart and Honey go all the way back home—and it'll take them longer because it's dark—then come all the way back here with help? I moved right up to the edge once and the ground held. Please let me try it again and go down to Janie."

"There's something in what she says," Dan told Jim reluctantly. "We can hold on to her from up here. She couldn't be in any real danger."

"He's right, Jim! Don't you see, Brian?" Trixie begged. "Jim, fasten the ropes to me, *please*. If it's all right to move Janie, we'll have her back up here faster'n you can say Voostenwalter Schimmelpennick!" Trixie was crying and laughing at the same time.

"Janie," she called, "are you all right?"

"Yes, Trixie," Janie called back, faintly. They could hardly hear her. "Dirt keeps falling. . . ."

"There's your answer," Trixie told Brian and Jim. "I'm not going to waste any more time. I'm going!"

Jim dropped his arms helplessly. "She might as well go. If we don't let her do it, she'll just take off into space, and darned if I don't believe she can even fly!"

Trixie, triumphant, held out her arms, and the boys fastened the ropes around her. They checked the other ends, looped tight around the trees. Then they watched as Trixie crept slowly—slowly—testing every few inches, crawling carefully till she reached the rim.

Slowly she dropped her feet over the edge. The ropes grew taut.

Down she went, dangling free, reaching for a foothold in the yellow clay of the cliff's sharp side—down, as the boys played out the ropes in response to her sharp tugs—down, till she stood on the jutting ledge where Janie lay, caught among the tough, thick branches of a cliffside pine.

"Janie," she cried, "Janie, are you all right?"

"I think . . . so. I can't seem to—to pull myself free. Oh, Trixie!"

"Thank heaven we found you," Trixie said fervently. "Don't struggle, Janie. Let me try to get you loose. No, no—just stay still while I pull on this biggest branch."

Carefully, gently, Trixie pried the gnarled pine branch away from Janie's imprisoned arms and legs.

"There," she said, putting her arm back of the girl's slight shoulders. "That old branch must have bruised and rubbed you terribly, but it *did* hold you, and it saved your life. There—can you sit up?"

Janie, stiff and weak, rose unsteadily to her knees, then rested a moment. Then, with Trixie's arm firmly around her waist, she stood erect, trying to repress a groan, her left arm drawn close to her body.

"Your arm . , . is it broken?" Trixie cried, frightened. "How can the boys pull you up?"

"It isn't my arm," Janie said quickly, "and nothing's broken. It's my wrist; it may be sprained."

"It will hurt dreadfully when you're lifted."

"Try me!" Janie said gallantly; then, with a rush of strength, she called up to the boys, "I'm ready to go!"

Nothing happened.

"Didn't they hear me?" Janie asked.

"I hope not. It's a good thing if they didn't. You don't even have the ropes tied under your arms. You see, they have to stand quite a way back from the edge. The rim of that bluff is eroded underneath. It wouldn't hold the boys' weight. It's as crumbly as a piece of cake."

"I found that out," Janie said in a trembling voice. "Wasn't I foolish? Trixie, you'll have to tie these ropes under my arms. I can't quite manage. But let's hurry before your flashlight goes out. Trixie, if any harm comes to you. . . ."

"It won't," Trixie said, her voice strong and confident. "I prayed my way down here, and I'll pray us both back to firm ground."

She tugged at the ropes till they were firm. "Thank heaven for Brian's Scout training. I'd never know how to make a running knot," Trixie said. "There you are, Janie. You're ready to go now."

Raising her head, Trixie whistled: *bob, bob-white!*

From above, the answering glad call came: *bob, bob-white!*

"Creep like a mouse when you go back up over

that brim," Trixie warned. "Safe landing!"

Without realizing it, she covered her eyes. *I'm
not going to look,* she thought as Janie's feet left
the ground. *I'll just stand here and do what I told
Janie I'd do—pray.*

For what seemed hours Trixie huddled against
the face of the rock, listening. She imagined she
heard scratching as Janie's reaching toes touched
the hard, rocky side and bounced away . . . imagined she heard the boys' measured panting as they
slowly, slowly strained at the ropes. She couldn't
possibly have heard that, of course, but in her mind
she followed Janie's ascent so intently. . . .

Bob, bob-white! The whistle came from above.
This was not imagination. This was a call of her
victory!

Janie was safe!

In a short time *bob, bob-white!* came again, and
Trixie deftly caught the rope dangling before her.
From above, well-known voices shouted encourage-
ment to her.

Mart and Honey were back! Help had arrived!

"Daddy is up there waiting," Trixie thought, "and
all the Bob-Whites!"

She didn't realize until she reached the top how
many people had rushed to the aid of a stricken,
nameless girl!

She hid her head on her father's shoulder as the
crowd cheered its tribute to her courage.

At Crabapple Farm, Trixie's mother opened the screen door and gathered her daughter and Janie into her eager arms.

"I couldn't believe you were both safe until I had you right here where you are now," she said, her trembling voice showing the tension she had endured. "Janie, you come back to your room with Dr. Gregory and me. Trixie, are you really all right? You aren't hurt in any way—"

"I'm not!" Trixie answered. "I just want to wash my face and hands and change my clothes. Moms, Janie is the bravest girl in the whole world."

"I have two brave girls, but, oh, Trixie, only my hairdresser will know, and she'll touch up the gray spots in my hair! You should leave that kind of exploit to the boys."

"Try and tell her that," Mart hooted.

"She saved my life," Janie said in a low voice. "I'll never be able to thank you, Trixie."

"I couldn't save you from all those scratches and bruises—and that wrist!"

"We'll take care of that now," Dr. Gregory said. "I'll have a report to make to Sergeant Molinson in the morning. If there was malicious intent in the removal of those signs, we'll have to know the reason. A second attack on the life of this harmless young girl is a disgrace to Sleepyside."

The crowd outside slowly dispersed. Dan left, too, as soon as he heard the doctor's report.

"There are some pretty ugly bruises," Dr. Gregory said, "and her left wrist is sprained. It could
have been so much worse."

"She was just beginning to recover from that
other accident," Trixie said, "and now this."

"She'll be over this in a few days," the doctor
said. "I wish I could say as much for her memory.
A jolt such as she had today could have helped to
restore it."

Honey sighed. "To think she doesn't even have
that to console her, after all she's been through!"

"I've given her a sedative. She was almost asleep
before I left the room, wasn't she, Mrs. Belden?"

"She was. Heavens, this group hasn't had a bite
to eat since goodness knows when. I'll just whip up
some batter, and we'll have waffles and bacon in
a few minutes. Won't you stay, Doctor? I'll start
the coffee perking."

"Thanks, but I'll be pushing on. I've patients
waiting in my office. Brian, you can rewind that
bandage on her wrist tomorrow. Let her sleep as
long as she will, Mrs. Belden. If she awakens and
seems restless, give her another of those small
white pills."

Brian, the future doctor, straightened in his
chair. "Dr. Gregory was pretty much rocked over
what happened to Janie," he said. "Who could
possibly have it in for a girl like her?"

Who? Trixie echoed the question in her mind.

*Who? We haven't a whisper of a clue. Tomorrow,
though, we'll talk to Sergeant Molinson.*

"Did anyone hear anything from Juliana today?"
Jim asked, interrupting Trixie's thoughts. "This
business of Janie put her clear out of my head."

Mrs. Belden clapped her hand over her mouth.
"Jim, I forgot! Juliana stopped in here about an
hour ago. She said she had been away from Mrs.
Vanderpoel's house all day. I promised her that
someone would call her and tell her about Janie.
Jim, will you please call? Use the phone on the
sun porch. It's quieter there. Have you beaten the
eggs, Trixie?"

"Yes, Moms. Di wants to make the salad. Where
is the lettuce hiding?"

"In the hydrator, where it always is. Brian, will
you mix some of that salad dressing you like? Jim—
Oh, he's telephoning. . . ."

"No, I'm not. Juliana wasn't home. Boy, does she
get around!"

"Maybe she got an answer to her letter," Honey
suggested.

"If she did, she didn't tell Mrs. Vanderpoel. She
hadn't even told her that Janie was lost. I guess
that gives us a pretty good idea how much she
cares about any of us."

Mrs. Belden put some plates to warm in the top
of the oven and turned around slowly. "It probably
means that Juliana has worries of her own." She

began pouring the batter. "Let's concentrate on supper now."

Soon hungry Bob-Whites descended on the stacked waffles, while Mrs. Belden kept the iron steaming and mixed another bowl of batter.

"Did Janie eat anything?" Honey asked.

"A bowl of soup, but her eyes were almost closing," Mrs. Belden answered. "Bobby will be cross when he knows we've had waffles. He loves them."

"My mom gave him his dinner at our house with the twins before I brought him home," Diana said. She laughed and went on, "I hate to tell you, but I ate dinner then, too; I never could resist waffles."

"It's a Belden specialty," Mr. Belden said and passed the jug of maple syrup to Diana at his side. "Bobby must have had quite a day. He was so tired he couldn't hold his head up. I let him climb into bed with his clothes on—even his shoes."

"You didn't!" Mrs. Belden said, more amused than shocked. "Brian, will you please answer the doorbell? Who could be stopping by now? One of the neighbors, I guess, to ask about Janie."

When Brian returned, Juliana was ahead of him. Her eyes traveled quickly around the group at the table. "Where's Janie? Nobody told me about her. Did you find her?"

"I tried to telephone you," Jim said, "but you weren't home."

"Janie's resting," Mrs. Belden explained. "She

had quite a fall. It's been quite a day for all of us. Will you have waffles, Juliana? There are hot ones just coming up."

Juliana shook her head.

"Or coffee? Or a piece of cake? I baked it while I was waiting for everyone to come back. I'd have lost my mind if I hadn't been able to do something."

Moms is talking too much, Trixie thought. *That means she's nervous. Juliana seems to do this to people.*

"I'm sorry I wasn't here to go with the rest of you," Juliana said, addressing her remark to Jim. "I've had things to attend to."

"Did you have an answer from Holland?"

"No, Jim, and I just *have* to have an answer pretty soon . . . very, very soon." Juliana's voice thinned. "Those thoughtless people in The Hague. No word at all!"

"Maybe you should have written to Mrs. Schimmel to take care of it for you," Trixie suggested. "She's right there in The Hague, as you know."

"Mrs. Schimmel? Who— Oh, yes, Mrs. Schimmel. I always called her by a pet name. She's far too busy." Juliana got up hurriedly. "If Janie seems to be all right, I'll go on. You don't need to go with me, Jim. I'll go by myself."

Mrs. Belden and the Bob-Whites followed her to the front door.

"It's getting late, Juliana," Mrs. Belden said,

"quite late, and it's dark. After Janie's experience.
. . . Don't you think Jim had better go with you?"

"No. I like the walk," Juliana said hastily. "This
isn't New York's Central Park, you know. It's the
little hick village of Sleepyside. I'll see you later."

Mart whistled. "She almost *blew* out the front
door. She's in a thing about something."

"Whether she wants it or not, I'm going to walk
along behind her," Jim announced. He closed the
screen door quietly. "We've had enough episodes
for one day."

Back in the kitchen, the Bob-Whites grew
quieter, realizing, finally, how tired they really
were. But, even so, the girls had the dishes done in
no time at all. Mr. and Mrs. Belden settled in the
living room to read.

"Stay with me tonight, Honey, please," Trixie
begged. "I'm still tingling. I can't sleep, I know.
We can talk—"

The door slammed. Jim came stalking in without
knocking.

"How do you like that?" he interrupted, sputter-
ing. "I'm the world's prize nitwit. I should have
known she wasn't walking home. It was that car
again—the green Buick—parked down the road. I
saw her get into it. Why couldn't she have said so?"

"Maybe she's going to give the Dutch lawyer the
heave-ho," Mart suggested. "Maybe she's found a
new love."

"She doesn't need to be so secretive about it. Who cares?" Trixie snorted. "Oh, Jim, I forgot. After all, she *is* your cousin."

"That doesn't keep me from wondering, too. Maybe she doesn't want Mrs. Vanderpoel to know. I don't know why she pussyfoots around the way she does. But, as your mom told me, it's really none of my business. I'm ready to call it a day. Come along, Honey. We'll take Di home. It's a shame Dan couldn't have stayed for some of those waffles, Mrs. Belden. Thanks a million."

"I think Honey will stay with me, Jim, maybe even for the weekend. She almost promised," Trixie told him.

"I'd love to, if you think Mom won't mind, Jim. Do you?"

"Have you ever known her to mind when you stay at Crabapple Farm? Come along, Di, you're stuck with me. I'll drive you home. I'll stop early in the morning, and we'll all go and talk with the police about those signs."

Brian and Mart went to their rooms.

Mrs. Belden went to Janie's room to check on her, then she and Mr. Belden said good night to Trixie and Honey.

Trixie let Reddy out and watched him go galloping around the yard. Then she and Honey went upstairs.

Report to Sergeant Molinson • 14

As THE STATION WAGON left Crabapple Farm the next morning to take the Bob-Whites to confer with Sergeant Molinson, Trixie said unexpectedly, "Let's stop at Mrs. Vanderpoel's house. Maybe Juliana would like to go with us."

Mart turned around and looked at her as though she had two heads.

Jim, surprised, said quickly, "Okay."

Dan Mangan, the most matter-of-fact member of the club, asked, "Why? She wasn't anyplace in the woods yesterday. She's never with us."

"Maybe that's why," Trixie said. "I've been thinking that we could have tried harder to be with her more. It's Janie's accident that threw us off—when she lost her memory and we brought her to live with us. I guess we just paid more attention to her because she seemed to need us more."

Juliana wasn't at home, as usual, when they stopped.

"She went out early this morning, about nine o'clock," Mrs. Vanderpoel said. "Come in, all of you. I haven't seen any of you but Jim for a long time. You must be pretty busy getting ready for the horse show at the Turf Club. That Regan is a slave driver, isn't he?"

Honey laughed. "Usually he is. He's been swell about our practicing lately. He and Dan give the horses a workout. We help when we can. It isn't often enough. Did you hear what happened yesterday, Mrs. Vanderpoel?"

"Yes, I did. Jim told me some of it. Then, when Juliana came home, she told me more. She seemed to be pretty badly disturbed about it."

Trixie raised her eyebrows. "She didn't show any sign of it when she stopped at our house. She hardly listened to anything we said about Janie's fall."

"Juliana doesn't show emotion. Dutch people don't." Then Mrs. Vanderpoel added, "Not on the surface, but we feel things deep down. I feel so sorry for that poor little nameless girl, Janie. I feel the same about you Bob-Whites, too. Your plans have had to take second place—your work at the hospital, helping at home, the Turf Show. Juliana is working on some dolls for a booth at the Show."

"Juliana?" Mart shouted. "Juliana working on a booth? She won't even be here. At least, I know she hopes she won't be here that long."

"I know that. She's pretty sure she won't be here, but she's making a lot of dolls—Dutch dolls—for the doll booth. Didn't any of you girls know it?"

Trixie, sobered and ashamed, shook her head.

"We didn't," Honey said.

"No, and I'd never have dreamed it," Diana said.

"That's what she does daytimes, mostly," Mrs. Vanderpoel told them. "She didn't tell me anything about what she was doing until yesterday. I thought you knew. I hope she won't mind my mentioning it now. She must have wanted to surprise you."

"Heavens!" Trixie said. "Think of it!"

"Every day she goes to work with some woman named Thompson. I don't know her. I think Juliana may have known her sister in the Bronx. This woman telephones to Juliana often. Her husband has been away, and she has time on her hands. She used to be a seamstress. I'll show you one of the dolls."

Mrs. Vanderpoel left the room.

"Boy, if that wasn't a blockbuster!" Mart said. He saw Jim's face and added quickly, "Well, did *you* think she'd make dolls for a booth? Did any of the rest of you think so?"

"See, isn't she pretty?" Mrs. Vanderpoel held up a little, flaxen-haired doll, its two yellow braids sticking out from an apple-cheeked rag face.

"She's darling!" Trixie and Honey said in unison.

"I guess we all need to take a second look at Juliana," Brian said slowly. "We've sure jumped to some wrong conclusions, Mrs. Vanderpoel."

"Maybe so. Maybe not. She puzzles me. I don't think she's happy. Maybe it's that business about the land that's worrying her, but she's up in the air one day and down the next. I think it's probably good for her to work with the dolls."

"Nights, too?" Jim asked, remembering. "Do they work on those dolls nights, too?"

"I guess they do. One of Mrs. Thompson's sons —I think—picks her up. He's been by several nights. I never see him. He just honks his automobile horn for her."

"Tell her we're so sorry we didn't get to see her on our way to talk to the police about those warning signs that were moved. We think someone did it on purpose, and that's why Janie fell."

"It doesn't seem possible anyone could be so cruel. You're right to try and track down who did it. This is more detective work for you, isn't it, Trixie?"

"If I can help," Trixie answered. "Oh, look at the time. It's almost noon. We'll see you later, Mrs. Vanderpoel. Be sure and tell Juliana we stopped by, and tell her we think it's simply super about the dolls. The only other booth we know anything about is the one Moms will have—the plant booth, with seedlings from her garden."

"Now, what do you think of that?" Trixie asked when they were once more on their way.

"I think we all need our heads examined," Mart said. "Moms kept telling us, one by one, that we should be more tolerant. . . ."

"Yeah. A fine bunch of Bob-Whites we turned out to be!" Brian said.

"It gives us something to shoot for in the future," Jim said.

Trixie, deep in thought, said to Honey, "It's the strangest thing—I wish I could remember where I've heard the name Thompson. Maybe Moms will know. Wasn't that the cutest doll?"

When Jim parked the car in front of the court-house, Trixie said, "I suppose Sergeant Molinson will be as impatient as he always is."

"Yeah," Mart answered. "He thinks you mess up his investigations and get in the way of his men when they're working on a case."

"She *does* get in the way," Honey said spiritedly. "And a good thing, too. All he has to do is to think back to some of the cases Trixie and I have helped to solve— Shhh . . . here we are!"

"Good morning, Trixie. Good morning, Honey. Good morning, boys. I'm glad you stopped in. I have some questions to ask you about what happened up there on the cliff yesterday."

"Did Dad see you this morning?" Jim asked.

"Yes. He's putting some men to work today to fence off that ledge where the girl fell. The erosion there has to be stopped, too. I have a call in for the county engineer right now. Trixie, although I still disapprove of your dangerous methods, you were a real heroine yesterday. If I have the story the way it happened."

"She was!" Honey said. "Trixie always does things nobody else has nerve enough to do."

"You're telling me!" the sergeant said.

"She finishes them, too," Honey said. "Sergeant Molinson, who do you think took those warning signs away from that place? Who is trying to injure Janie?"

"Wait just a minute, young lady. Those warning signs having been removed doesn't necessarily mean that someone wanted the girl to fall over the cliff, does it?"

"What other possible reason?" Trixie asked.

"Maybe the county engineer's department was making some kind of a survey before undertaking anti-erosion work there. The signs may have been in their way."

"So they threw them over the cliff?" Trixie asked. "That doesn't wash."

"How do you know anyone threw them over the

cliff?" the police sergeant asked.

"Because," Jim said, "we found them down below, smashed. We think someone moved them on purpose."

"Yes, we do," Trixie agreed. "And if you'll give me a chance, I'll tell you about a lot of other odd things that have been happening. Some strange man was hanging around the surveyors. Some strange man put our station wagon out of commission in the Bronx. Some strange man was parked near our house the night—"

"What on earth does that have to do with the young girl Janie?" Sergeant Molinson said, smiling indulgently and sending a crimson flush to Trixie's cheeks.

"There *is* some connection someplace. An important police officer like you should find it. You just get me all confused. Anyway, with all the experts working on the case, nobody yet has been able to find out what or who hit Janie and left her unconscious."

"These things aren't accomplished in a day, Trixie. We have to have time."

"And nobody has the slightest notion what her name is, where she came from, or who her family is," Trixie went on. "It's awfully hard on Janie not to know." Trixie's voice saddened, remembering Janie's bewilderment.

"That, too, takes time, Trixie."

"In the meantime, some terrible thing is going to happen to her. I *know* someone is trying to harm her. They've tried twice—once when they left her unconscious on Glen Road, when she lost her memory, and yesterday, when she fell. Who knows? Maybe the next time they'll succeed. Isn't there *something* someone can do?"

"Trixie, we don't just sit here and twiddle our thumbs."

"I'm sorry."

"Sit down here, now, all of you. Tell me exactly what happened yesterday. Begin at the first, when you missed Janie. Tell me in detail. You start, Trixie."

Trixie started. When she came to the place where she went over the cliff, Jim took over.

The sergeant listened intently. He asked questions at intervals, then sat back and listened again, glancing from time to time at Trixie.

"Then we pulled Trixie back, as slowly as we possibly could. We were scared to death that edge would give way with her. But it didn't!" Jim finished triumphantly.

Sergeant Molinson said sternly, "Trixie, I'm wasting my breath, but I'm strongly advising you to be careful, to leave perilous adventures such as yesterday's to people whose job it is to do them."

"I was right there," Trixie said. "It had to be done then."

Sergeant Molinson threw up his hands. "I give up. At least three people have been to see the mayor today about a medal for bravery for you, Trixie."

Trixie gasped.

"She deserves it," the sergeant told the other Bob-Whites. "I'll have to admit she gets in my hair; nevertheless, I could name some of my men who could use a little of Detective Belden's perseverance and inquisitive turn of mind. Remember this, Trixie," he continued, "we're doing everything in our power to investigate every facet of Janie's case. It's a matter of the greatest concern to my department."

"I know it is," Trixie said. "Thank you, Sergeant Molinson."

Spider Kicks Up a Clue • 15

JEEPERS!" Trixie said as they left the sergeant's office. "Did you hear what he called me? 'Detective Belden.' This must be his 'be kind to people day.' It's the first time I've ever left his office without being shushed out. Oh-oh . . . here it comes now."

Sergeant Molinson opened his door and called down the hall. "Jim!"

"Yes, sir?"

"Will you, to save us all from going crazy, see if you can keep that cousin of yours from haunting this courthouse? She's here when we open in the morning and here when we close. She's driving the recorder of deeds nuts."

"Yes, sir, I'll try . . . I mean . . . well, we'll try."

"I see what you mean."

"His 'kind to people day' didn't last long, did it, Trix?" Jim asked. "How can Juliana haunt the courthouse, when she's busy every day sewing on those dolls?"

"She probably does ask every morning," Trixie answered. "They've told her they'll let her know as soon as the papers arrive. Why do you suppose she's in such a frantic rush?"

Mart shrugged his shoulders. "Search me! It could be she doesn't like this 'little hick town' of Sleepyside."

"Could be." Brian agreed. "What now?"

"How about hamburgers down at Wimpy's?" Jim suggested.

"That's an idea!" Mart seconded. "It seems as though we never have time for Wimpy's anymore—not since school closed, anyway. Remember the old days, when we'd run into Spider Webster?"

"Oh, yes!" Trixie cried. "I *wish* Spider were on the police force here now. I suppose he did want to take a job with more money, and that's why he went to White Plains. We never see him anymore."

"Speak of the devil!" Mart cried. "Do you see who's right inside that window? Spider! Hi!" he called, waving.

Eagerly the Bob-Whites crowded through the door. Spider, grinning from ear to ear, shook hands with each one as they came through. "Say, this is great!" he said. "It's like old times. Every time I used to have a lunch break, I'd run into one or more of you kids here. Let's line up at the counter again, huh?"

"Our treat!" Jim said. Then he called out, "Mike, hamburgers, french fries, and malts for all of us. Say, Spider, how have you been? Where's Tad?"

"My brother is working at a summer camp up-state in the woods. Say, I never have stopped being grateful to you Bob-Whites for the way you helped me straighten Tad out."

"Don't say a word about it," Brian said. "Mrs. Vanderpoel misses both of you a lot."

"And do we ever miss her cooking! Boy! I hear she has some dame staying with her now—the one who inherited that strip of marsh where they're going to build the factory." He whistled. "Nice little sum of money she'll get for that . . . one hundred and fifty thousand dollars!"

"How come you know all about that, when you're never in Sleepyside anymore?" Jim asked. "She's my cousin, you know."

"I know that, too. I was in Molinson's office on business this morning, and she had just been in the recorder's office inquiring about something. You know Molinson; he doesn't like dames too well, huh, Trixie?"

"Now he does. Now he doesn't," Mart said. "This

morning he almost pinned a medal on Trix."

"I heard about that rescue, too. Say, Trixie, that
was some stunt you pulled up there on the bluff.
That girl who lost her memory is staying at your
house, isn't she? Makes a guy believe in miracles
to look up at that bluff and think she wasn't—"

"Murdered!" Trixie said grimly. "That's what it
was, Spider—an attempt at murder. The second
one, too. How did you know about Janie—we call
her Janie—"

"I saw the poster in the Missing Persons Bureau
in White Plains. I didn't connect it with you Bob-
Whites till I stopped at the station today. When I
talked to the sergeant, I found out this Janie is
staying at Crabapple Farm. There's no news of
who she really is, is there? Has the sergeant any
clue to how she came to be on Glen Road? Hit-and-
run, was it? What a shame!"

"It's tragic, Spider," Honey said. "She's the
loveliest girl."

"It's awfully sad." Trixie's face grew solemn as
she thought about Janie's predicament. "I *wish* we
could help find out who she is."

"Sometimes they just disappear, girls and boys,
grown men and women, too," Spider said, "and no
one ever hears a word about them."

"Does it happen the other way, too?" Trixie
asked. "When nobody ever makes an inquiry about
a missing person?"

"Often," Spider said, "but it's mostly some no-good bum nobody wants to find, someone like that stepfather of yours, Jim. Nobody cried up a storm when he disappeared, did they? I guess he knows better than to show his face around these parts again."

"No fear," Mart said. "When he realized he wasn't going to get anything out of Mr. Frayne's estate, that it all went to Jim, he beat it."

Spider laughed. "It's a good thing he did, or he'd have landed in the clink, with a good push from me. What are you kids up to? I'll give one guess. Trixie and Honey are on the trail of that hit-and-run criminal and are now trying to figure out what happened yesterday. Right, Trixie?"

"We are concentrating on trying to find Janie's identity," Trixie said. "We didn't think we could do much about what caused her accident on Glen Road. Then a lot of other things began to happen, Spider. Yesterday was the worst. We're certain that someone is trying to harm Janie."

"Do you have any idea why?"

"No, we don't. We're completely baffled. Someone is definitely out to get Janie. I don't think Sergeant Molinson agrees with us yet about this. He's trying to discover who moved those warning signs yesterday. He thinks the workmen who have been busy there may have done it, that maybe it has nothing to do with Janie. I don't. I have a hunch."

"I'd bank on your hunches, Trixie. I've had experience with them before."

"Tell it to the sergeant," Mart suggested.

"He's had experience with them, too. You say he's trying to find out if someone moved the warning signs, and if they did, why. Do you mean the signs along that trail in the woods?"

"Yes. They were in place a little over a week ago when we were riding through the woods, exercising the horses. That's when we found out about the factory that's to be built. We climbed down that path to the marsh. . . . Oh, Spider, I do wish you were on the police force in Sleepyside now. You wouldn't keep saying, 'It all takes time,' the way Sergeant Molinson does. You'd move."

"Do you want me to go with you now and take a look around that cliff? Not that I'd be likely to find a thing, because investigation really does take time, Trixie, as the sergeant said. I'm taking the rest of the afternoon off. We can run out to the woods. Maybe I can stop and see Mrs. Vanderpoel, too."

"Would you, Spider? That would be super. Has everyone finished eating? Brian, how about settling with Jim for our hamburgers?"

"You forgot I said it was my treat, Trixie—on account of Spider," Jim said. He paid the bill, and they went out.

"You haven't seen the new Bob-White bus, have

you, Spider? Well, open your eyes and look!" Mart opened the station wagon door with a flourish. "Our name's on it, and everything."

Spider looked, struck his forehead, and fell back, as though dazzled.

"Have you been picking up some more rewards, you and Honey?" he asked Trixie. "Boy, oh, boy, is it ever snazzy!"

"Mr. Wheeler gave it to us. They have a new Continental sedan," Trixie said.

"I might have known it came from him." Spider whistled. "I wish all kids had the setup the Bob-Whites have—your own clubhouse, and now your own car. Not that you don't have it all coming to you, always trying to help people. Let's see how the Bob-White bus rides."

Jim stopped the car on Glen Road where the trail entered the woods, and they all got out. As they neared the end of the bridle path, they could hear the sound of men working, voices shouting, hammers pounding.

"It's the men putting up the guard fence my dad ordered," Jim said. "It sure didn't take long to get them going."

"Money makes the mare go," Spider said. "That's what my old daddy used to tell me when he tried to make me save. No kidding, Jim, when your dad wants a thing done, it's as good as done. I wish we could have come up here before they got under way, though. There isn't much chance of finding anything significant now; probably never was."

"It's a ghastly place over there," Trixie said, pointing to where the shelf of soil was breaking away. "It didn't used to be that bad when we went down to the marsh for specimens. At least, I don't remember it being scary. We've climbed down that path often enough."

"I always thought your stepfather escaped this way, Jim, after your great-uncle's house was burned. That old river has provided a getaway for many a crook, with all the boats and barges lined up down there. Hey, you!" he called to one of the workmen. "Is this a hole where one of the warning signs was in place?"

"I don't know. Ask the county engineer. They're puttin' up new signs. We're buildin' this fence right across the path where you're standin'. Can't nobody go beyond there then. We're gonna paint KEEP OUT! in red paint on the fence when we're done."

"It seems to me it needs a sign here, too, at the top of this trail down to the river," Spider said, pointing to the hole, widened and gaping where a sign had been hastily pulled up.

Absentmindedly he kicked the dirt with his heel, to cover up the hole, and uncovered a tobacco can. He picked it up and tossed it over to the workman. "Here's your tobacco," he called. "One of you must have dropped it. What's the matter, Trixie?"

"Nothing . . . I guess. That's horrible smelling tobacco, isn't it? Some of it spilled here."

"It wouldn't be my choice, but that's why they make all kinds. Well, kids, it doesn't look as though there's anything I can do around here. I'm sorry, Trixie. Even if we'd come to this place earlier, we wouldn't have found clues on all the bushes. A smart cookie covers his tracks pretty well."

"We didn't really expect to find anything incriminating, did we, Trixie?" Honey asked sadly.

Trixie didn't answer. Her mind seemed miles away.

"How about you kids stopping at Mrs. Vanderpoel's house with me for a while. Do you have time to do that—then run me back into Sleepyside?" Spider asked.

"I suppose we should be exercising the horses for Regan," Jim said, "but the day's already pretty well shot."

"And Mrs. Vanderpoel always has cookies," Mart said, smacking his lips.

"She's the best cook in Westchester County," Spider said, "and that takes in a lot of good Dutch cooks. Many a time I've wished Tad and I were back at her house and pulling up to that kitchen table."

It wasn't long till Spider's wish was fulfilled. When they dropped the knocker at the little,

yellow brick house, Mrs. Vanderpoel opened the
door, cried out with delight, and put her arms
around Spider.

"You're my wish come true, Spider!" she said.
"Do you know what I have in the oven?"

"Cookies!" Mart said.

"Oh, those! I always have those. No, sir, it's
Spider's favorite food. Mr. Maypenny brought me
three pheasants today, all dressed so nice and
pretty. I cut them up, browned them, covered them
with sour cream, and popped them in the oven. I
was going to freeze them, because they wouldn't
keep till Juliana and I finished eating them. Come
right in, all of you. Do you smell them cooking?"

"Mmmm! Mmmmm. I'm back where I belong,"
Spider said, drawing in his breath. "Does that ever
smell good to me!"

"There's enough for everyone," Mrs. Vanderpoel
said hospitably. "Stay for dinner, all of you. I was
afraid there would be nobody but me. Juliana's not
here for dinner; she's working on those dolls," she
added, looking at the girls.

"I should be at home helping Moms," Trixie said.

"And I should be at home with you, helping you
help your mom," Honey said. "Oh, Trixie, that
divine smell!"

"If I call Moms and she says yes, and if you'll let
us help get dinner, and if you really want us—"

"Trixie means yes, we'd love to stay, and when

do we eat?" Mart said. "I'll call Moms." Soon he
reported, "She said yes."

"I'll call Miss Trask and tell her where I am and
not to look for me. If she knows we're with you,
Spider, she'll want to visit with you, too," Jim said.

"Later on. Later on. Soon we eat, though," Mrs.
Vanderpoel said. "Set the table, please, girls. Here's
the cloth."

"One, two, three, four, five, six, seven of us,"
Trixie counted. "Jeepers! Nobody else in the world
could have six extra people walk in on them and
provide a banquet."

"In the old country, yes," Mrs. Vanderpoel said.
"My mother told me that many a time on Sunday,
after church, someone would say, 'Come to dinner,'
and they'd come, and welcome, too. My mother was
a good cook. Her mother was, too."

"They'd have to have been, to have taught
you," Spider said. "I'm telling you the truth. I wake
up in the night, and I can taste chicken and dump-
lings and apple pie and Gouda cheese—thin slices
of it on toast in the morning instead of butter—
mmmm! I'll bet when Tad writes to you, Mrs.
Vanderpoel, he always mentions food."

"He does. I do miss both my boys, Spider. Even
Old Brom looks around the corners hunting for you
whenever he comes into the house. As soon as I
whip up these potatoes, we'll be ready to eat.
There's new late corn from my garden in that pot

on the back of the stove. My, but it seems good to have all of you here!"

"I wish Janie could be with us, too. She's so thin, but she's never hungry." Trixie sighed.

"There'll be plenty of pheasant for you to take home to her, Trixie, and some for Bobby, too, the little darling. There, now, you can fill the mugs with milk, Honey. Spider, you can take this platter to the table. Put it right in the middle, and you can all help yourselves. See what a big pan of pheasant I have?"

They all ate till they could hardly push back from the table. Mrs. Vanderpoel wouldn't let the girls help with the dishes. "It'll keep me busy after you've all gone," she said. "The evenings are too long. I'll just fix up a bit for you to take to Janie and Bobby, and I'll put the rest away . . . maybe leave a little in the warming oven for Juliana, if she comes."

She scurried about the kitchen, and in no time at all the big table was cleared and the dishes scraped and piled for washing later.

A delicious bouquet of odors filled the big old-fashioned kitchen—an aroma that never left it—made up of scrubbed cleanliness, lingering spices, tangy pickles, ripe apples, crumbling aged cheese. Over all, and enhancing all, was the spirit of whole-hearted hospitality and love.

Afterward, in the cozy parlor, Mart picked out

lively rock music on Mrs. Vanderpoel's beautiful little melodion. They clapped and hummed and shuffled their feet.

"Dance, if you want to," Mrs. Vanderpoel urged. "Nothing can harm an Axminster carpet. Nothing has for forty years."

So Spider swung the rotund little Dutch woman to her feet and whirled her around the room, while the others snapped their fingers or shrugged and twisted to Mart's one-fingered beat.

In the midst of it all, in walked Juliana.

She nodded to the Bob-Whites. Then she saw Spider. His blue suit and brass buttons seemed to paralyze her. "A policeman!" she gasped.

"A friendly one," Spider said, bowing low.

"It's Spider. I've told you about him," Mrs. Vanderpoel said. "It's Juliana, Spider, Jim's cousin. I've kept something warm for you, dear. The Bob-Whites and Spider all stayed for dinner. I wish you had been here. Were you working on your dolls again?"

Juliana hesitated, then nodded her head.

"You make me ashamed, Juliana," Trixie said. "We haven't done a thing about booths for the Turf Show. We love the dolls you're making. They're darling."

"Thank you," Juliana said nervously. "If you will excuse me, I'll go to my room. I'm glad to have met Mrs. Vanderpoel's Spider. I'm glad to have seen the rest of you, too. I hope Janie is feeling better. I'll say good night now."

She spoke it as if it were a piece she had learned, Trixie thought. *She's terribly nervous. She had such a queer smile . . . or . . . there goes my imagination again!*

Aloud she said, "I think we have to say good night, too, Mrs. Vanderpoel." She hugged the roly-poly woman with both arms. Honey did, too. Even the boys, Mart shamefacedly at first, then whole-heartedly, hugged her.

"It's no good saying thanks. That word couldn't cover the wonderful time we've had," Trixie said from the doorway.

"Don't say it. Come again. That's the thanks I like best. Good night, now, all of you."

At Crabapple Farm, where Jim let the Beldens and Honey out of the station wagon, they said good night to Spider.

"I'm sorry I couldn't help you with your sleuthing, Trixie," he said, and she knew he really meant it from his heart. Then he added, chuckling, "I just happened to remember—I saw a couple of your good friends in Sleepyside today. Snipe Thompson and his nephew Bull. I guess their time is up in the pen. They probably won't try to rob another antique show, Trixie, but they're bad citizens—mighty bad citizens. Good night."

A Shadow at the Window · 16

SEE WHAT I brought you, Janie! Moms, where's Bobby? Has he gone to bed? Mrs. Vanderpoel sent him some pheasant, too. Get a whiff of this, Janie!"

Trixie uncovered the bowl, still warm.

"Mmmmm . . . mmmmm, delicious! Bobby went to bed only a minute ago. Please, Mrs. Belden, may he come downstairs?"

"If you'll promise to eat every bit of your share. You hardly ate a thing for dinner," she replied.

"Oh, dear!" Trixie said. "We were all wishing so much that you could be at Mrs. Vanderpoel's house. We ate and ate and ate. She's almost as good a cook as you are, Moms."

"Flattery! Flattery! Here comes Bobby. He heard his name."

"I smelled something good."

"You couldn't possibly eat, after the way you crammed yourself at dinner."

"I can *always* eat. Mmmm . . . pheasant! Here, you have some, too, Moms . . . just a little bite. Daddy?"

"Who do you suppose was at Mrs. Vanderpoel's house with us this evening? Guess!" Trixie's eyes shone.

"Spider!" Bobby shouted.

"Who told you?"

"Mart did." Bobby giggled. "Mart did, when he told Moms you could stay at Mrs. Vanderpoel's house for dinner. I wish Spider was still living in that house, Trixie."

"So does he, Bobby. I don't think he's too happy in his job at White Plains, do you, Honey?"

"Nobody who's ever lived in Sleepyside is completely happy anywhere else. I know I'd never be."

"Mrs. Vanderpoel wishes Spider still lived with her, too. You know, Moms, it's kind of scary back there in the woods. I keep remembering the time I stayed there all night, and Snipe and his nephew tried to rob the place."

Mrs. Belden smiled. "It seems funny now, but it was frightening at the time. I don't like to think of it. The funny part was the way Mrs. Vanderpoel was ready for the thieves. Isn't she wonderful?"

Trixie giggled. "She took down her father's old rifle and aimed it at them and said she'd shoot their heads off if they came an inch closer."

Mrs. Belden's face became sober. "They *could* have shot first. The situations you get yourself into, Trixie—you and Honey!"

"They scare me to pieces, too, Mrs. Belden," Honey said. "But Trixie always gets us out of danger, someway."

"Maybe she does, but I keep thinking the time will come when she won't. I suppose you and Spider had a big fun time talking over all that's happened."

"We did," Trixie said. "I told him all about the things that are puzzling us and all about Janie."

Mrs. Belden looked at Janie and saw her face sadden. "Did he have any suggestions to make?"

"Not a thing," Honey said. "He wanted to. He even went with us up to the trail in the woods. He thought he might possibly find some kind of a clue. He didn't, though. The men were working there on the fence Daddy ordered them to build. All Spider turned up was an old, half-filled tobacco can . . . ugh!"

Trixie shuddered, too, at the memory of that awful-smelling tobacco . . . and something else. *Where did I smell that very same smell? Someplace before the Bronx. Where was it? It was someplace I hated. I was afraid....* "What did you say, Moms?"

Mrs. Belden busied herself clearing up the dishes they had used, rinsing them, setting them aside to be washed in the morning. "I said we'd better all make this an early-to-bed night. Skip along, Bobby. I don't think anyone in this house slept well last night, after that terrible day we had."

"We'll go in a minute, Moms," Mart said. "I just want Janie to pick out the melody of that song she sang. I don't mean the King Arthur one—the other one." Mart hummed. "I was trying to remember it at Mrs. Vanderpoel's." He went ahead of Janie into the living room and handed her his guitar. "How did it go, Janie?"

"I'll just play the tune on one string. It'll be easier for you to remember if I don't chord it. Listen, Mart. It's in F sharp:

> " 'Down in the churchyard,
>   All covered with snow,
>   My true love's a-lying.
>   Hang your head low.
>   Mourn for my true love,
>   Under the snow,
>   Mourn for my sweet love.
>   Hang your head low.' "

Mr. Belden looked up from his newspaper. "Can't you think of something less mournful?"

Mart hummed, trying to harmonize with Janie.

"What did you say, Dad? Oh, blast! There's the telephone."

"I'll get it," Brian called.

Trixie could hear his voice on the kitchen extension. He must be talking to Jim. Something was "swell."

"What was it?" she asked Brian when he came into the room. "What was so swell?"

"It was Jim. When he took Spider back to the police station, where he'd left his patrol car, Jim saw Sergeant Molinson just leaving. He said he guessed Jim's cousin was happy now, since those papers she'd been waiting for so long had arrived and she had finished her business at the courthouse."

"Gol . . . I'm sure glad for her," Mart said. "I guess I'm glad for everyone concerned. But, say . . . that's funny. . . ."

"What's funny, Mart?" Janie asked and put down the guitar.

"We saw her just a short time ago at Mrs. Vanderpoel's . . . Juliana. . . ."

"We did," Trixie cried, "and she didn't say one thing about getting those papers."

"Maybe she didn't know it then," Brian said.

Mart jumped up from his chair. "Hey, maybe she didn't. Trixie, why don't you go and call her?"

"At this hour?" Mrs. Belden asked.

"She knew it, all right," Trixie said. "I'm not

going to call her and get squelched. Don't you remember how she was so high-hat and said she was 'going to my room'? If she'd wanted us to know, she'd have said so. She sure blows hot and cold."

"Remember about the dolls," Honey said.

"That's the only 'blowing hot' she's done that I can remember. I can remember plenty of 'blowing cold' times— Why do you suppose Reddy is barking so much?"

"He's off on a rabbit's trail," Mr. Belden said.

"I guess I'm jittery," Trixie said. "Honey, shall we go to bed? You aren't the only one who's yawning. Look at Brian!"

In her room, Trixie turned on the pink-shaded lights on her dressing table and found a pair of pajamas for Honey.

"These are your best ones!" Honey protested.

"So what? You're my best friend."

"Okay, as long as you put it that way. . . . Trixie?"

"Yes?"

"I wish I could warm up to Juliana more. I can't. Can you?"

"Huh-uh." Trixie stopped brushing her short curls. "I can't. Every time I think she's getting a little human, she does an about-face. Why do you suppose she didn't tell us that she had heard from Holland?"

"I don't know. She talked about it enough before," Honey said.

"And she acted so funny at Mrs. Vanderpoel's, and she hardly ever says anything really kind."

"That Mrs. Schimmel who raised her, though," Honey put in, "told us she had grown to love Juliana like her own child. And Mrs. Hendricks, the neighbor in the Bronx, said some pretty nice things about her, too!"

"So did her little boy." Trixie's face was thoughtful. "Kids never pretend. They like people right away, or they don't, and no fooling. Look at Bobby."

Honey nodded. "He's not one of Juliana's fans."

"I'll say he isn't. He's crazy about Janie, though."

"I wonder. . . ." Honey picked up the brush Trixie had abandoned and ran it the length of her honey-colored hair. "One, two, three." She counted as she stroked.

"Honey?" Trixie said.

"Yes?"

"Do you think we've been fair to Juliana?"

"You mean we've been too quick to see her faults?"

"That, and maybe, because Janie was in the hospital . . . maybe we only thought about her."

"Maybe so. I suppose, now that she's heard from Holland, she'll be off to the Poconos. I wish, for Jim's sake, we had been nicer. He hasn't seemed too keen about her himself, though, especially lately."

"It's because he thinks she's double-crossing that lawyer in The Hague she's supposed to be engaged to."

"That *is* her own business. I guess falling in love isn't all moonlight and soft music and roses. Maybe a person can make a mistake, Trixie."

"She did grow up with that lawyer in The Hague. She should have been sure."

"Mmm-hmm," Honey mused. "Sorta like you and Jim, maybe."

Trixie blushed. It was one thing for her to think deep in her inmost thoughts that Jim was someone superspecial, but it was another thing to say it aloud. Ever since they'd first found Jim, she and Honey, and saved him from that old Jones, his stepfather— How *could* Jim's mother ever have married a man who even *looked* like Jones? Sleek, city-slicker type, coal black hair, a crooked gash for a mouth. On TV and in the movies, women did seem to fall for a crooked smile.

"Have you gone into a trance?"

Honey's voice startled Trixie out of her reverie. "My mind was wandering," she said.

"I'll say. To go back to Juliana—we're always finding something to criticize. I move we accent the positive from now on, maybe have a big party for her at our house before she goes. Shake?"

Trixie put out her hand. "Shake."

Honey yawned and slipped under the covers.

Trixie put out the light, then sat on the edge of her bed, thinking.

There was no sound save Honey's even breathing. Honey must have gone right to sleep, Trixie thought. Finally she, too, lifted the light cover, swung her feet, and slid under— What was that sound? It was smothered . . . stifled. And it seemed to come from downstairs.

Janie's room was downstairs. Was something wrong with her?

Trixie found her slippers. "If I turn on the light, it will waken Honey," she thought. "It's probably just my imagination. It's been that kind of a day."

Reaching out her hand, she followed the wall to the door, then went softly down the hall, her footsteps not making a sound on the carpeted floor. Downstairs, she went through the living room and dining room and down the back hall to Janie's door.

The sound came from there, unmistakably. Janie was sobbing.

Trixie opened the door, went over to Janie's bed, and dropped to her knees beside it. "What is it, Janie?" she whispered. "Is it pain from the bruises? Does your wrist hurt?"

"Oh, Trixie," Janie said, tears half choking her voice, "*who* am I? Won't I ever find out?"

"Of course you will," Trixie murmured, her arm reaching comfortingly around Janie's shoulders. They were such thin, frail shoulders.

"Just you wait, Janie. Do you know what sometimes makes me wake in the night and sit right up
straight? It's the thought that suddenly, suddenly
someday, you will remember; then the people you
belong to will take you away from here. We'll all
miss you so much, Janie."

Janie sniffed and took the tissue Trixie pushed
into her hand. "I know that, Trixie. In the daytime I
feel warm and loved, secure and safe, but in the
night. . . ."

"In the night it's harder, I know." Trixie slipped
into the bathroom, brought back a cool cloth, and
ran it over Janie's face. "I brought one of those pills
Dr. Gregory gave you to help you sleep. Here, sip
this water."

Trixie waited while she swallowed the sedative.
In the faint moonlight that came from the window,
her poor scratched face looked so forlorn. A shadow
moved across it. A shadow from where? Outside?
Perhaps from the curtain stirring in the breeze?
Suddenly uneasy, Trixie went to the window and
looked out. Seeing nothing but the garden, peaceful
under the moon, she returned to Janie.

"There, now, go to sleep." Trixie tucked the sheet
around Janie's shoulders. "Who knows? Tomorrow
may bring an answer to all our questions."

Softly she tiptoed to the door. There was no
sound, no sound anywhere now, except Janie's
even breathing as the pill took over.

Something Curious About the Dog • 17

POOR JANIE," Trixie thought as she crept back into bed. "Nobody seems to be doing one thing to help her, and she *is* in dreadful danger! Spider seemed to be sure of this. He couldn't do anything to help, either. It's the most mixed-up puzzle. I wish Janie's problems could be solved the way Juliana's seem to have been."

From the next bed Honey's breathing rose and fell in quiet sleep.

Outside, the moon had disappeared. Intermittent yellow heat lightning flickered. There was silence ... silence everywhere.

Finally Trixie, too, slept.

Bong!

Trixie, startled, sat bolt upright in her bed.

Bong! Bong! Bong! Three times more. Somberly
the grandfather's clock in the downstairs hall had
announced the hour of four.

Somewhere outside, a branch broke. Lightning
sent its pale, trembling light across the room.
Thunder followed, distant, low, long, rumbling.

Silence.

Across the yard, out of the silence, something
stirred and crackled in the shrubbery.

Trixie listened.

There it was again . . . that noise. A strange dog?
No. Reddy would have routed another dog with his
barking.

Almost as eerie as the rustling sound itself
was the light that came and went through the open
window. That shadow she saw in Janie's room—
the shadow that crossed in the moonlight—was it
really a shadow?

Dread quickened Trixie's heartbeat. *Janie!*

Pushing her toes into her slippers, she tiptoed
down the hall. "Shall I waken the boys?" she wondered. Noiselessly she opened their door a crack.
They were *so* sound asleep. "If I call them," she
thought, "Bobby will wake up, then Moms and
Dad. There'll be bedlam, because Bobby will howl.
He always does when he's awakened suddenly
from a sound sleep.

"I'll get my robe and slip downstairs by myself. No, I'll wake Honey. If I don't let her go with me, she'll never forgive me. She won't make a sound if I shake her just a little."

"What is it?" Honey whispered through Trixie's hand held over her mouth. "What time is it? What do you want, Trixie? What's wrong?"

"That's what I want you to help me find out. Get your slippers and robe. I think something queer is going on outside. Shhh! We mustn't wake everyone!"

"What did you see? What did you hear?" Honey asked sleepily.

Trixie told her. "It's not much, I know. I don't *think* that I imagined that shadow when I was with Janie."

"And you think we should go . . . outside . . . alone? It's dark. There isn't even any moonlight now. Ohhhhh . . . listen to the thunder! Trixie, I'm not going out there, and neither are you. There's no reason to be scared of anything. Reddy would have been barking like fury if anyone were prowling around. I guess you didn't think of that, huh?"

"I did," Trixie whispered. "I thought the same as you, that Reddy would be watching. Then I remembered some lines I read in a mystery book. One of the detectives said, speaking of a scary time like this, 'There was a curious thing about the dog that night.'

"The other detective said, 'The dog did nothing that night.'

"Then the first detective said, 'That was the curious thing.'

"Honey, I've always remembered those words. Tonight it's curious about Reddy. Where is he? *We have to find out what is going on.*"

"Why can't we call the boys and your father?"

"And wake everyone? Give the prowlers a chance to get away? Honey, it's our one chance . . . maybe . . . to help Janie, to find out—"

"But I'm scared to death!"

"Honey Wheeler, what possible danger could we be in? We're right in my very own house in my very own yard with my very own dad and brothers right near. Jeepers, are you going with me or not?"

"You know I am. I always do. That doesn't mean that I'm not shaking all over. Where are we going?"

"To the garage. We can slip out the back door and over there. We can see the whole yard from that little window on the landing leading to the haymow. Thank goodness for that window. Our garage used to be a barn, remember. *If* I'm right, and *if* someone's prowling around, we can call to Dad and the boys. Let's go!"

Trixie took Honey's hand and led the way in the darkness.

Down the stairs they stole, out the back door, then, between lightning flashes, into the garage.

Click! The door slammed.

"It's the wind," Trixie told Honey. "It's getting stronger."

From their post at the window, they saw jagged heat lightning cut across the garden. Thunder muttered after it. A pine at the corner of the garage scratched ominously.

Honey shivered. Her teeth chattered. "It's so creepy out here, Trixie. Can't we—"

"Sh!" Trixie warned. "Look!" A chill rippled along her spine.

Across the vegetable garden, near the fence, the shrubbery stirred before their watching eyes— stirred, then parted!

A dark shape emerged, crouching, creeping, scuttling, running—straight toward the house and Janie's window!

"Quick!" Trixie gasped. "Let's call my dad. *Daddy! Daddy! Daddy!*"

"*Help!*" Honey echoed. "*Help! Help! Help!*"

Their voices seemed lost in the thunder.

They rushed down the stairs and pulled at the garage door.

"It's locked!" Trixie cried desperately. "Help me pull, Honey!"

"I *am* helping! Oh . . . Trixie . . . we . . . can't . . . get . . . out!"

"Yes, we can! The door locked itself. I heard it click when we came in. Oh, Honey, *that man's*

going straight to Janie's window! Yell! Yell like you
never yelled before! Darn that thunder. Nobody
can hear us! Yell! Pound! Pound hard on the door.
Push! Let's both push together. Push hard with
your shoulders. Push!"

Wham!

The door gave way, sending them sprawling.
Trixie jumped up, then pulled Honey to her feet,
and they ran, shouting, *"Help! Help! Help!"*

Halfway to the house, Trixie saw the man turn
and look back. Just then a flash of lightning picked
out his features. Black, shining hair gleamed. From
a crooked, contorted mouth, a hoarse voice snarled,
"You!"

"It's Jim's stepfather!" Trixie gasped. "Daddy!
Daddy! Daddy!"

Why didn't *someone* turn on the lights in the
house?

Why didn't *someone* hear their cries?

Oh, why didn't *someone* come to catch that man
before he got away?

Had he drugged everyone? *Was . . . everyone
. . . in . . . that . . . house. . . .*

In her agony, Trixie heard the sound of a starting motor, saw a red taillight disappear down Glen
Road, and saw the car swallowed up in tree-
shrouded darkness.

Simultaneously the commotion inside the house
became bedlam . . . a combination of falling furni-

ture, cries of "Where are the lights?" Bobby's shrieks, doors slamming, and rushing feet.

"Where are you, Trixie?" her father's voice called.

"Trixie!" Brian echoed.

Mart's and her mother's voices, high with fright, called, "Trixie!"

"Here!" Trixie and Honey called. "Turn on the garage light!"

"The lights are all out, all over the house. What *is* happening?"

"He must have cut the wires!"

"Who? Stop muttering, Trixie, and pull yourself together." Mr. Belden held his daughter close to stop her shaking. "There, now, tell me . . . *who cut the wires?*"

"Jim's stepfather. We saw him. He came here to harm Janie. He was . . . going . . . toward . . . her window! Oh, Daddy!"

"Harm Janie? Jones? Why?"

"I don't know. Daddy, *where is Janie?*"

"I'm here, Trixie. Who is Jones?"

"Thank heaven you're all right, Janie. Daddy, where's Reddy?"

"Here," Brian said grimly, "not twenty feet from the garage. Asleep . . . drugged."

"Here's the thing that did it!" Mart cried, from near Janie's window, holding up a shiny object. "Jim's stepfather was going to drug Janie. Why?"

"The sheriff will have to find out," said Trixie,
her voice shaking.

It was almost daylight before the sheriff arrived.
The telephone lines to Crabapple Farm also had
been cut, so Mart and Brian ran to Manor House.
Soon the whole area was alerted.

Lights flashed on in houses.

Jim, Brian, and Mart took off down Glen Road.
Their search was in vain, for Jones had been clever.
Cut wires had given him a start that would be im-
possible to overcome.

Voices, voices everywhere. Trucks and cars ar-
riving. Trucks and cars leaving. Men from the telephone company, urged on by the police, repaired
the cut lines. Electric power came back to the
house. A veterinarian arrived to care for Reddy.

A bright sun followed the night's storm. A warm
wind blew in from the south.

Dan, summoned by Jim, arrived from Mr. Maypenny's cottage. He had stopped for Diana and
brought her with him. They were told of the night's
events.

Mrs. Belden, capable as usual, busied herself
getting breakfast.

"Set ten places at the table, Trixie," she said.
"The girls will help you pour orange juice. Will it
be pancakes or waffles or scrambled eggs?"

"Eggs and bacon," Mr. Belden said. "Then you

can sit at the table with us. It keeps you from hopping from stove to table with waffles or pancakes. Will that be all right, gang?"

"Anything to fill us up, Mrs. Belden. I wonder what it would take to knock out our appetites." Jim brought paper napkins from the box over the refrigerator and pushed chairs up to the extended kitchen table.

"Somebody make the toast," he said as Diana set mats at each place.

"Toast coming up!" Brian said. "Jim, you get the telephone. It sounds like long distance—you know, more mechanical, longer rings—"

"I'll take it," Trixie said eagerly. "Maybe it's a report from the sheriff. Hello? Oh, Mrs. Hendricks. It's that neighbor next door in the Bronx, next to the De Jongs' house," she explained to the others hurriedly. "Yes, Mrs. Hendricks? *He did?* This morning? Didn't anyone know he was coming? Oh, Juliana will be delirious when I tell her. Yes, ma'am, she's been here all this time waiting for some papers. I think they came yesterday. I'll call her right away. Tell Hans we'll go with Juliana to meet him at the bus in Sleepyside. Yes, probably in about an hour. We'll check with the bus station about the time of arrival. I can't wait till we telephone the news to Juliana."

"Now, guess what?" she asked as she returned the receiver to the hook.

"Juliana's fiancé must have arrived from Holland. He's the only Hans connected with Juliana that we've heard about," Mart said. "I'm not as sure as you seem to be that his coming will be so welcome."

"Why not?" Honey asked.

"She's had this other guy on the string, too."

"Mart Belden, you sure don't keep your ears open. Don't you remember? Mrs. Vanderpoel explained that Juliana was working on those dolls. That was what took her away from the house all the time. Juliana went to Mrs. Thompson's house to work, and it was her son or nephew or somebody who came after Juliana in the car. Besides," Honey added quietly, "I thought we decided not to be imagining everything."

"Gosh, Honey, you're right," Mart said. "Trixie, are you going to call Juliana?"

"Trixie's already on the phone," Bobby said, "the one in the living room. Listen! Boy! Listen to her! She sounds pretty mad."

"Now what can we tell Hans Vorwald?" Trixie sputtered as she came back into the room. "Juliana isn't there. She left early this morning. That isn't all. Mrs. Vanderpoel said she took everything she owned with her. So she evidently didn't intend to come back. She didn't even say good-bye to any of us—not even Jim. Do you think we should try and reach her fiancé in the Bronx?"

"He must be halfway here by now," Jim said. "I can't believe it! Juliana *must* have intended to see us before she left. I wonder who called for her at Mrs. Vanderpoel's house."

"The faithful Thompson relative," Trixie said, "of course— Say . . . wait a minute . . . wait!"

Two things hammered at Trixie's brain: "Thompson" and "all of her things are gone."

A clear, bright light broke.

With a cry, Trixie jumped to her feet. "I may be the biggest idiot in the world—or the smartest detective in the state of New York!"

"Is there a choice?" Mart teased. "Say, Trixie, where are you going?"

Trixie opened the screen door. "Don't ask any questions, any of you, *please*. Come with me to the bus station, *please!* All the Bob-Whites! Jim, drive as fast as you can! There isn't much traffic. Hurry, please, Jim!"

The Bob-Whites didn't ask questions. They followed Trixie. They all piled into the station wagon, and Jim was off, with a screech of tires, down Glen Road toward Sleepyside.

Just outside the village, Trixie, sitting on the edge of the seat next to Jim, ordered, "To the bank first! Oh, I hope we're in time! Wait for me!"

In a few minutes she was back, her face grim with disappointment.

"Juliana cashed that check for a hundred and

fifty thousand dollars less than an hour ago. She *had* to have made arrangements days ago for that big a sum of money to be ready. How dumb I've been!"

"So that's what my stepfather has been hanging around this vicinity for. Trust him to try to get in on that kind of money! He may even have kidnapped Juliana!"

Trixie didn't answer. "To the sheriff's office now, please, Jim," she directed. She stopped but a moment there, ran out, jumped back into the car, and said, "To the bus station now, please, Jim. Keep the engine running, and I'll go in and meet Hans."

"You?" Mart asked. "What's all the high-handed business about, Trixie? Don't you think we're smart enough to be in on it?"

"Mart," Trixie begged, "for a little while longer, please trust me. I don't have time to say anything else, but I'm right! I know I'm right! You wait and see. Now, Jim, park right here and keep the engine running. I hope Hans is on that bus that just arrived. Keep your fingers crossed!" Trixie was out of the car like a flash.

In a few minutes she came back with a tall, handsome, blond young man.

"This is Hans," she explained and motioned him into the seat next to Jim. Then she crowded in after him.

"Whirl around, Jim, and go back to our house!"

"Our house?" Mart asked, bewildered.

"Oh, Mart," Trixie begged. "Our house," she repeated to Jim, "and fast!"

Jim stepped on the gas, backed around, and was off. Trixie, from the front seat, tried to introduce the Bob-Whites to the dazed young man from Holland. Then, when he didn't seem to be making sense out of anything, she shrugged her shoulders with a gesture of frustration and said, "Wait! That's all I ask of any of you. Wait! In about three minutes you'll know the score."

Up the road the Bob-White station wagon flew, turned into the driveway at Crabapple Farm, and screamed to a stop.

Mr. and Mrs. Belden and Bobby, with Reddy at his heels, ran out. Janie followed slowly.

Trixie got out of the front seat. The young man from Holland followed.

When Janie saw him, a blazing smile swept over her face. With a cry of joy she rushed into his arms.

"Hans!"

"*Juliana!*"

Hans caught her close to him, spun her off the ground, set her back on her feet, looked at her searchingly, and asked, "Juliana, *why* didn't you write to me? I was crazy with worry. I couldn't wait any longer. I had to come to the States to find out what kept you from writing. Why didn't you write, Juliana?"

"*Juliana?*" Jim echoed. "She's Juliana?"

"Juliana?" the confused Bob-Whites repeated, looking to Trixie for an answer. "Janie is Juliana?"

Exultant, clapping her hands, Trixie nodded toward Hans and Janie. "Just listen to what she's saying," she cried. "*She is Juliana.* She's been Juliana all the time. She's telling him about her accident on Glen Road and how she lost her memory. Listen! *Janie's memory has come back!*"

Janie Remembers! • 18

In the living room, with the Bob-Whites, Trixie's mother and father, and Bobby listening, Janie told Hans her story.

"I wrote to you from the De Jongs' home about seeing my mother's name in a newspaper article. It told of some land in Sleepyside, owned by Betje Maasden, my mother. I was all ready to go to the Poconos with the De Jong family for a vacation. Instead of going with them, I decided to go first to Sleepyside, find out about the land, then join them later."

"You didn't write me about your change of plans, Juliana," Hans said. "The last I heard from you was the letter about the article in the New York City newspaper."

"I didn't write because I fully expected to send a letter to you from Sleepyside and tell you what I had discovered here."

"When I didn't hear, and didn't hear . . . oh, Juliana, I've been desperate. I tried calling on the transcontinental telephone, but there was no answer." Hans's voice was troubled. "Your wrist is bandaged! Your face is scratched. Did you fall?"

Trixie sat on the edge of her chair, listening. *This is Janie remembering!* she thought.

"I drove my own car, my blue Volkswagen," Janie hurried on, aware of Hans's concern. "It was when I reached the outskirts of Sleepyside, after I left the highway. I remember thinking what a pretty little city it was, but what a lonesome stretch of road! I . . . I . . . ."

Janie shivered, hesitated.

Oh, don't let her stop remembering now, Trixie prayed, eyes closed.

"Go on," Hans urged and put his arm around his fiancée's shoulders. "Go on, Juliana!"

"I hadn't gone far, when a man stepped in front of me . . . an evil-looking man. I'll never forget his face as long as I live. Shiny black hair and a cruel, crooked mouth, tobacco-yellowed teeth—"

"My stepfather!" Jim groaned.

That terrible smelly tobacco, Trixie thought.

How could I ever forget it?

"He held out his hand to stop me. I *had* to stop, or I'd have run right into him. I remember twisting the steering wheel to pass him, but I lost control of the car and headed straight for a tree. . . ."

Janie paused, her voice choked with tears. Then she went on. "That's all I remember, Hans, till I awakened in the hospital. Oh, Hans, everyone has been so good to me. I couldn't remember my name. I couldn't even remember *you*, till I saw you get out of the station wagon."

"She tried so hard," Trixie said. "Every time she tried, that phony Juliana—I wonder where she came from and who she is—every time Janie was on the edge of remembering, that awful girl tried harder to keep her from remembering."

"How could we have been so simpleminded?" Jim said disgustedly. "My phony cousin is off with all that money that belongs to Janie . . . nobody knows where . . . while we've been sitting here like a bunch of dumb clucks, letting her get a head start."

"I don't think so," Trixie said quietly. "Do you remember the stop I made at the sheriff's office before we went to the bus?"

"You were *that* sure, Trix?" Jim said. "I guess you weren't one of us dumb clucks."

Trixie grinned. "Go on, Janie. Hans will want to know everything. Oh, Janie, it's so wonderful to know finally that you can remember!"

With words tumbling over one another, Janie told of the hospital, the Candy Stripers, Dr. Gregory, the nurses, the Bob-Whites, their club and their station wagon, Mrs. Belden, and her stay at Crabapple Farm.

At this point, Trixie and Honey took over, with help from the other Bob-Whites. They told of the man at the marsh, the letter from Mrs. Schimmel, the trip to the Bronx, the mysterious damage to their car, and the appearance at Mrs. Vanderpoel's home of the phony Juliana.

"What happened to my darling little blue Volkswagen?" Janie interrupted.

"I guess the police will have to figure that one out," Jim answered. "All we want is a chance at that stepfather of mine!"

"You said it!" Brian agreed. "When I think of the next trick he pulled, when Janie fell over that cliff!"

Hans gasped, and an answering groan went up from the Bob-Whites.

After they had told Hans this part of the story, he asked, "Didn't anyone suspect your stepfather, Jim?"

"How could we at that point?" Trixie broke in. "He hadn't been seen around here for two years— not since he tried to get Jim's inheritance away from him. For a detective, I was a prize dumb bunny. In all the cases Honey and I have worked on, there never have been so many mixed-up happenings and clues that we missed."

"You were not aware that 'Janie' was really my Juliana, Trixie, so how could you solve so many mysteries? Oh, Juliana, to think of all these things threatening you, with me halfway across the world."

"You are here now," Janie said, smiling up at him. "Think of the good friends I've had, not even knowing who I was. I think the Bob-Whites and their parents and all their relatives and friends are the kindest, best people in the whole world."

"We're so kind that we almost let you get murdered last night," Trixie said. "I don't know why my mind didn't click when I heard Mrs. Vanderpoel say that Juliana had been with the Thompson family."

"Yeah," Mart said. "You sure had reason to remember Snipe Thompson. That name should have set off an alarm."

"How many bells have been ringing in *your* head?" Brian asked Mart. "Trixie and Honey didn't know Jones was even in these parts, till they saw him when the lightning flashed last night. They were up and on the watch. You and I were snoring in our beds."

"I'm getting confused," Hans admitted, smiling for the first time since he had heard of Janie's accident. "Can someone 'cue me in.'"

In chronological order, then, the Bob-Whites told the whole sordid story as far as they knew it.

As they neared the end, the telephone rang.

Trixie answered. It was the sheriff. She talked for a minute, then turned to the listeners.

"He says he has a couple of interesting customers in jail—Jones and his niece. Spider Webster helped bring them in. He saw the green Buick parked in White Plains. The sheriff is getting a tape recording of their story. The girl was sullen and clammed up, hasn't said a word. Jones was mouthy, as usual. The sheriff wants to know if we'd like to listen in on a playback of the tape about an hour from now, when he's hustled them off to maximum security. People in Sleepyside are pretty well worked up. Spider and Sergeant Molinson's men have jailed Snipe Thompson, his wife, and his nephew for questioning. Shall I say we'll be down there in about an hour?"

"Right!" the Bob-Whites agreed.

"Moms, I'm hungry!" Bobby cried and wondered why everyone laughed.

"Come to think of it, fella, so am I," Brian told his little brother. "Moms?"

"I know." Mrs. Belden hurried to the kitchen. "Hamburgers for everyone. Hans must be very hungry."

Hans, deep in low conversation with Janie, didn't answer.

Sometime later, in the sheriff's office, the Bob-Whites, with Janie and Hans, watched the deputy slip in the tape and adjust the recorder, heard the sheriff's questions, and listened to Jim's stepfather's answers.

They heard him tell of seeing the story in the New York newspaper and remembering that his wife's sister had been named Betje Maasden. *If* this were true, he had thought, he might be in for some big money out of the deal.

Disguising his voice, he had tried to make a call to Jim to verify the name. Failing to reach Jim, he'd hung around the marsh, trying to pump some information out of the workers there. They had run him out. Then he went to the courthouse and tried to put in a claim, but they told him they wouldn't make a move till they had more information.

So he watched the Sleepyside newspaper for more news and learned of Mrs. Schimmel's letter from Holland *and* of the little Juliana's survival after her mother and father had been drowned. He learned, too, that the girl, now grown up, was in the Bronx at the De Jong home, and that if she made a claim for the land, she would inherit it.

Fortunately, his niece—

"This is where the phony Juliana comes in," Trixie whispered to Jim.

"Shhh!" he answered. "Listen to the tape."

". . . impersonate her," the tape continued. Jim's

stepfather's voice droned on sullenly, while he explained how he planned to kidnap the girl and substitute his niece for her.

He'd gone to the Bronx ahead of the Bob-Whites, and, though Juliana had left there, he hid in the shrubbery, learned that she had been driving a blue Volkswagen, and heard Honey tell the neighbor of the route the Bob-Whites would follow going back to Sleepyside. It was okay with him when they went into the neighbor's house for Cokes and cookies, because it gave him a chance to vandalize the station wagon and get a head start on the trail of Juliana.

He had only intended to waylay her, kidnap her, and hold her captive at Mrs. Thompson's house, then substitute his niece until the deal was concluded and the money paid.

However, Juliana's car had hit a tree. When she was knocked out, he had thought she was dead.

So he took her car and all her identification and hid out at Snipe Thompson's, and his niece took over. She was a pretty good actress, wasn't she?

"No, she wasn't," Trixie said out loud. "I should have known she couldn't possibly be Jim's cousin and be so mean. I'll bet she never made but one doll . . . just to throw us off."

"Shhhh!"

When he learned the girl wasn't dead, but only unconscious, and that she had lost her memory, he still went ahead with his plan, hoping time would be on his side and the money his before she recovered her memory.

"You even tried murder twice," the sheriff's voice cut in, contemptuously.

"If it had to be. Time was getting short," Jones answered. "A hundred and a half grand ain't picked up on just any old street. I'd have gotten away with it, too, if that outfit that call themselves the 'Bob-Whites'—and mostly that girl Trixie Belden—hadn't been in my hair.

"Snipe and I had a good trap laid up there on that cliff. He got rid of the signs. . . ."

"And another attempt at murder last night, with your drug that almost killed the Belden dog. That was meant for the real heiress to the money, wasn't it?"

"Yeah, but that nosy kid, that amateur dick—"

"She saved my life!" Janie cried and ran to put her arms around Trixie. "She and Honey—oh, and all the rest of them there on the cliff. It has been so terrible, so horrible. . . ." Janie's lovely eyes were clouded. Then they grew bright as stars. "But think of the friends I've made!"

"They are the best in the world," Hans said devoutly and added, laughing, "I know they can't all possibly come to Holland for our wedding, Juliana. Maybe I can make arrangements through the Dutch consulate so that we can be married here in

Sleepyside, then spend our honeymoon in those
mountains where you were going . . . the Poconos?"

"Oh, *please* have your wedding at Crabapple
Farm!" Trixie shouted.

"How about having it at Manor House?" Jim
asked. "Janie is my cousin, you know."

"That's right, at Manor House," Trixie agreed.

Janie clapped her hands, color flooding her
lovely face. "Perfect! Trixie must be my maid of
honor, and Honey and Diana must be my brides-
maids. We must invite Spider Webster and his
brother and dear Mrs. Vanderpoel—"

"I don't know who they are," Hans said, laughing. "I'll learn. If they are friends of yours, Juliana,
they will be friends of mine, too. Jim must be my
best man, and Brian, Mart, and Dan ushers," Hans
added. "Bobby must carry the ring."

Trixie's eyes shone. Who would have dreamed it
would all turn out like this, after all the horrible
things they had endured? Janie looked so pretty,
and as for her handsome fiancé, Hans. . . .

"We'll be so busy," she said excitedly. "We'll
have such loads of things to do to get ready! Janie?"

"Yes, Trixie?"

"I've never in my whole life ever been anyone's
maid of honor! I've never even been a bridesmaid,"
she added. "Jeepers, imagine! Me!"